# QUEEN OF ASHES AND SCARS

### A DARK FANTASY ROMANCE

## THRONE OF SHADOWS
### BOOK TWO

## ANYA J COSGROVE

Queen of Ashes and Scars

Cover designer: Fiona Jayde Media

Queen of Ashes and Scars/Anya J Cosgrove

ISBN 978-1-7381056-4-9

✿ Created with Vellum

# PLAYLIST

Queen of Kings - Alessandra
Children of the Revolution - Bono
Bad Romance - Thirty Second to Mars
Vow - Garbage
King - Florence and the Machine
Angels with Dirty Faces - Sum 41

## CHAPTER I
# DEAD BLOOMS
### ARIELLE

"Long live the Dark Queen," Alec declares, the statement heavy with consequences.

He's kneeling in front of me like his life is now mine to command, and my undead heart beats in my throat. The others-— Leo, Lucas, Jude, and Keenan—freeze at the news, and I clench a hand around the train of my dress.

The living room and balcony of the Pereira's guest wing served as a dressing room for a wedding that will no longer take place. It's big enough for all of us to fit in, but way too small for all the wild emotions running through my body.

The somber faces of my entourage riddle me with goosebumps. I came to this court to marry a man I now consider to be a vile, unworthy king, to become his queen—but I could never have imagined this. My family used to rule the world, but now... now I'm not sure I'll survive the night.

Lucas shifts from one foot to the other, looking as uncomfortable as he did yesterday when he told me we were *just* friends. "Are you sure he's dead? Sebastian isn't exactly the most reliable witness."

My ex best-friend looks brittle next to Jude. The discreet bodyguard is quiet and rooted to his spot next to the door leading to the corridor.

Alec's golden-rimmed eyes narrow, his annoyance with Lucas obvious. "Yes, I'm sure."

Swallowing back fresh, useless tears, I grip the ugly necklace my betrothed tried to enslave me with. It's still stuck around my neck, and the news of my brother's passing makes the snare feel heavier still.

"How did he die?" I ask.

Alec's gaze dips to the ground. "Victor was murdered by a Zhaos' assassin at the airfield. He was on his way to the wedding. Peter Chastain was with him and barely got out alive."

Leo reaches for my hand, and I hold on tight, afraid I'll sink if I don't. His support keeps me from spinning out of control, the anxious pulse in my belly threatening to overwhelm my senses. Hunger itches at the back of my throat, my instincts to hold on to my first-blood and never let go, almost short-circuiting my rational brain.

*If Pereira has his way, Leo will die tonight...*

I can't let that happen.

Keenan clears his throat loudly. The drop-dead-gorgeous, blue-eyed angel mercenary was hired by Pereira to kill Leo and keep tabs on me, but he turned over to our side—at least for now. He spins around to face the window, his apparent flair for the dramatics on full display. A white aura shines around him, and his chestnut curls sway to an unfelt wind as he gazes into the distance. "Your Majesty, we have maybe fifteen minutes before everyone in this mansion learns that yer brother is dead and that ye are the queen of the Delacroix's empire. The Pereiras will not let ye leave. If they were enthusiastic about the wedding before, they'll do *anything* to make it happen now."

"Hell, *they* might have had your brother killed," Alec adds with a sad pout.

The last hints of twilight color the top of the quiet mountains, the city lights now visible in the distance as Keenan turns back to face me, and my turmoil is swallowed by his thrall.

The peace rolling off him is more soothing than a mother's embrace, and I squint at him, wondering just how much he can influence my mood. "What do you propose?"

"We have to get ye out, and quickly." His simple white t-shirt and faded-blue jeans somehow enhance his god-like quality, and the foreboding in his voice scatters chills along my spine.

The tall, broad-shouldered angel might have switched sides, but I know so little about him still... The suspicion in my gut makes his crafted, cottony warmth fizzle out a bit. I can't afford to check out and curl up in this stranger's embrace, but it terrifies me to no end that his powers are strong enough to make me wonder just how sweet my life could be if I kept him by my side forever.

Alec nudges me back to reality, his hand brushing my waist. "First thing first. Let's get you out of this dress."

"Yes, *please*." My stomach gives a big squeeze as he rips the white fabric off me, the corset underneath delicate enough to count as undergarments.

Alec presses his lips together, his eyes so dark that I wonder if he's the same man I exchanged so many quips with last night. Over the last few weeks, I've grown increasingly familiar with the masculine angles of his jaw and the deadly shape of his shoulders, and yet I'm not sure I recognize him now.

He looks simply murderous, ready to burn down the entire world for his queen. "We will need to get out through the servant's exit without being recognized," he says quietly.

Lucas steps forward, bursting into the protective bubble created by Leo and Alec. "There's a throng of caterers, blood-slaves, and the odd guest using the servants' stairways to hop outside for a smoke. I think it can be done."

"Jude. Get Bella, and ask her to come at once. Alone," Alec orders.

The royal guard obeys and comes back less than a minute later with Bella in tow. My stylist raises an alarmed brow at my discarded dress. "What can I do for you, princess?" she asks without hesitation.

"We have to get our new queen out of here." Alec points between the two of us. "You two should switch dresses."

Bella unzips the side of her black dress hurriedly and passes it to me without question. The simple black v-neck garment is easy to slip on, and I tie my hair in a tight bun at the back of my neck.

A pair of black sunglasses, strappy heels, and a red scarf meant to cover my neck the way the blood slaves cover their bite marks complete the look.

Bella tries to remove the necklace and fails at it, too, so she adjusts the scarf to cover it instead, her top lip curled in a sneer. "How can we get rid of that *thing*?"

I shake my head. "We can't trust any of the witches or warlocks here, so we'll worry about this wretched collar later."

While we were changing, Alec and Lucas also switched tuxes. Lucas' black jacket and simple white undershirt is less recognizable and conspicuous than the Delacroix royal guard uniform, but it's slightly too small for Alec, and he curses under his breath.

Jude helps Bella into my wedding dress. "I'll escort Bella out to the balcony for a few minutes. From a distance, it'll seem as though the princess is catching her breath outside."

Alec grips his colleague's arm. "Alright, but no more than five or six minutes, or you won't make it out."

Jude's mouth twitches. "This is no worse than Berlin."

"*Nothing* beats Berlin," Alec cracks up, lines visible at the corner of his golden-rimmed eyes for a split second before the focussed mask of the royal guard returns. "Safe travels, my friend. We'll disappear into the city and regroup at the airport."

Lucas raises a shaky hand to his brow. "The king has eyes and ears everywhere. They'll be watching the airports, so you should try a boat instead."

"Boats are slow."

"Bite me, Beaumont." Lucas snaps, all fake pretenses forgotten.

I lay a hand on both their forearms to stop the testosterone showdown.

Keenan and Alec stare at each other in silence for three whole seconds before the angel says, "Ye heard the kid. We'll find a boat." He drags his thumb across his bottom lip, moving closer to my first-blood. "Leo will come with me. I can get him out."

My first-blood swallows hard, the bob of his throat visible before he squeezes my hand. "Alright."

I hug Leo goodbye, drawing in a deep breath to imprint his scent in my memory. I don't want for us to go our separate ways, but he's probably got a better shot at making it out with Keenan than me. "I'll see you soon."

"Be careful." He holds me to him for a moment, and butterflies flutter in my stomach at the weight of his touch and the obvious affection in his quiet plea.

"I'll stay here and stall them as long as possible when they come knocking," Lucas says, his pout telegraphing exactly how uncomfortable he feels to be stuck in the middle of this conflict.

"Goodbye, Lucas." I peck his cheeks for old times' sake. The space behind my eyes tingles, the eerie intuition that I'll never see him again stealing my breath. A week ago, I would have begged him to come along, but the rift between us seems too wide now. I'm not the meek girl he once kissed. I'm not afraid to break the rules or voice my opinions, and I don't ever want to be herded into a sheep mentality again.

Jude steps onto the balcony with Bella as Alec and I slip out of the room. My royal guard's body is coiled like a well-oiled machine, ready to run and strike down my enemies, so I quickly check the empty hallway and pull him to a stop.

"Relax, you look like fucking James Bond," I scold.

Alec glowers at my jab but shakes his nerves loose, looking slightly less threatening. "Act hungover, and hold onto my arm like I just fed from you all night."

I grin at the double-entendre. "Didn't you?"

Warmth touches his eyes for the first time since he heard the news of my brother's death, and a tingle of affection quakes through me. "Don't tease me right now, Lucky. I'm trying to save your life."

We descend the servant's staircase and cross paths with one of the Pereira's handmaids. I force a stupid, dreamy smile on my face and hang from Alec's arm. The fiend squeezes my ass, the motion so crude that I struggle to hold in a gasp. The woman keeps her gaze down, her wrinkled nose betraying a hint of judgment, and Alec offers me a satisfied smile.

We pick up the pace and glide along the white hallways and stairwells, only slowing down when we hear someone coming. Thankfully, most of the staff members are busy carrying in flowers, gifts, or cutlery for the reception, but Alec still takes advantage of every single one of these encounters to grope me, the shameless way he handles my body setting me ablaze.

We're playing at blood-slave and master, and while this court's customs disgust me, my body has other ideas... When I first turned into a vampire, my flesh howled for blood. Now, it seems that my cells crave Alec's touch beyond reason, and despite the gravity of the situation, I wish I had enough time to take a bite out of him.

As we near the corridors leading to the kitchens, Alec flattens me to the wall and buries his face in my neck to avoid the scrutiny of yet another passerby, and my lids flutter. There's a certain...desperation in his performance, as though he's holding me for the last time. His hands grip my waist over the fabric, his teeth dragging across my jugular, and the man grins as he walks past us.

"Oh, God," I groan for effect, not having to fake the desire in my voice.

A wave of molten heat engulfs me, and Alec waits a few seconds before sliding back. His hold grows heavier on my shoulders for the last few yards, and by the time we hurry down the steps to the servants' side entrance, we no longer have to pretend to be a couple looking for privacy. I'm simply boiling inside, ready to burst. "Was that really necessary?"

"Absolutely," he answers with more verve than I expected. "You're Queen now. I might never get the chance to touch you again."

"Is that so?" I arch a playful brow, but something brittle in his voice tells me we're no longer playing games. Does he think so little of me that I would forsake him now that I'm in charge?

*And where does all that heat come from anyway?*

Before I can ask him to elaborate on his comment, he clasps my hand hard. A few arriving guests stand merely a hundred feet away from us on the outside curb in front of the mansion. A line of flashy cars has formed beyond the red carpet of the main entrance, their drivers being greeted one by one by the valets. Alec and I take advantage of the crowd to cross the slick stretch of black asphalt and head for the parking garage.

*"What the fuck? What is the princess doing out here?"* I hear in my head, the crystal-clear thought coming from someone close-by.

I dig the balls of my feet into the ground, pulling Alec to a stop, and search the covered porch. "Wait. There!" I motion to a vampire slipping back into the driver seat of his sports car, "He recognized me."

Alec jolts into action, and my vampire senses boom to life, following his sleek, soundless movements as he wrenches open the car door and slaps the man's phone out of his hands. The driver opens his mouth to speak, but Alec slits his throat with a long, aconite-coated blade. He's both stealthy and efficient, and my heart races at the sight of him so...ferocious. The vampire explodes in a cloud of dust, and Alec takes his place behind the wheel. He picks up the dead guy's cellphone and cancels the outgoing call. "Perfect timing, my queen."

My blood runs a tinge hotter and thicker, the predator in me pleased and excited. Without missing a beat, I walk around the car and climb into the passenger seat. "Drive."

The tires screech along the asphalt as Alec slams down the accelerator, a cloud of smoke rising in our wake. We whizz through the winding path leading to the main road, and my blood ices as we approach the guarded checkpoint.

A line of about a dozen cars has formed outside the gates, and four guards are chatting with the drivers, probably checking their identity before letting them in.

"Should we slow down?" I ask, quickly calculating our chances that they won't look too closely at us or report our unscheduled, ill-timed exit.

Alec reaches over his left shoulder. "Fasten your seatbelt, Lucky."

## CHAPTER 2

# INESCAPABLE

## LEO

I stand rigid next to the door leading to the balcony while Lucas Pereira paces the length of the dressing room back and forth. The air thickened after the princess' departure, and we're counting down the seconds before we make our own attempt at escape.

Keenan tucks his phone inside the back pocket of his blue jeans and follows Lucas' nervous movements the way a cat watches a wild bird. His brown curls lick the top of his ears, a stubble visible on his jaw, and I find myself staring at him. The calm he exudes is more addictive than any drug.

"What makes you so sure you can get me out?" I ask him quietly, thinking about the silent conversation I caught between him and Alec Beaumont. "I'm as good as dead, aren't I? You just needed her to leave with him? Don't sugar-coat it for me, I'm okay with it, really."

"Don't be ridiculous. I'll get ye out without a hitch, Leo." His loose grin grates my temper, his confidence somehow more unnerving than if he'd just explain what's about to happen.

Ever since Jorge called my name on that step in Hadria, a part of me has been wishing for death. Now that the only thing standing between me and eternal sleep is something corrupt about my DNA, it puts things into perspective. The angel might be on our side for now, but only because he plans to turn me into one of his kind-—a demon with a special taste for dying men.

"I saw you and Alec Beaumont... You made a secret agreement, didn't you?"

Keenan leans into my ear, the slight motion somehow making him look even taller than he is. We're pretty much the same height, but his powers give off a vibe that makes me feel all vulnerable and...human.

"We did make an agreement, but not about you." Dark wings flicker at the man's back, and before I can blink, Lucas Pereira falls to the ground, knocked unconscious by a surgical blow to the head. Keenan's grin widens. "I don't trust this guy. I think he was planning to rat us out as soon as we left the room."

I stare at Lucas' unconscious form, a hint of relief sizzling through my gut. "I agree."

Keenan lifts his chin to the balcony, interrupting my inner musings. "Those two should really get going."

Bella strips from the half-torn wedding dress and slips on Jude's discarded jacket. The royal guard opens the door for her, the human woman a shade whiter than usual as they leave. They've got the best chance of making it out, being less high-profile than the rest of us, but I wonder if I'll ever see them—or Arielle—again.

A full minute passes before Keenan presses a hand on my shoulder, melting the distance between us to a mere inch, and a shiver shakes me from head to toe. Being touched by an angel is comparable to being lulled to sleep by your lover's embrace. Even if you don't want to lose your bearings—maybe you have a full day in front of you, or in my case, your fucking life hangs in the balance—you still curl up into them and wish you could stay there forever.

His hot breath caresses the shell of my ear. "You will walk downstairs to your room and wait for me there. In exactly three minutes, I will blink in and bite yer neck." The rogue curve of his mouth quickens my pulse. "Ye're allowed to fight a little."

*Three minutes...*

Cold sweat sticks to my back as I obey his orders, my heart pounding in my ears, and I decide he shouldn't have told me about his plan. Every vampire I cross paths with shoots me a predatory look, my palms sweaty as hell. I'm a walking bag of blood, and my quickened pulse attracts too much attention.

Arielle feeding on me was one thing, but the thought of Keenan tasting me...of me fighting him *a little*...

*Two minutes.*

I close my bedroom door behind me and lean against it, my chest heaving. My nails grate the wood at my back as I take stock of my possessions and quickly decide I don't need to pack anything. I was allowed to bring a few trinkets from my old life but I obstinately refused, so all my things are new and devoid of sentimentality.

*One minute.*

A servant runs down the corridor, and loud chatter erupts into my bubble.

*They know about the escape, about me. It's all over. Whatever happens next, I can't let them use me to get her back, so a quick death might be for the best...*

Keenan blinks inside the room—I knew he was coming, and yet I gasp when he appears. My fists clench at my sides as I ponder what kind of fight he expects, and what fighting him *a little* actually entails.

I don't know what I expected. I thought he would pounce on me the way Arielle did the first night, and I was prepared to resist, half of it for show, half of it because of the gut-wrenching fear twisting my insides. But all the vampire bites I've heard about or lived through couldn't have prepared me for an angel's kiss.

Keenan glides towards me, the lull of his powers like wraith hands prying out my heart and leaving a hollow space in its place.

The emptiness is filled with a desperate need for him, an eerie warmth that erases all thoughts of others.

Dark, velvety wings flicker at his back, and my breath catches in my throat.

*So beautiful.*

*An angel of death.*

He cradles my head with his big hands, and my knees wobble, my whole body held upright by the thread of his touch. My stomach flip-flops as our noses touch. Hope and sorrow mingle on his breath, his eyes bluer and deeper than a pure summer sky.

I open my mouth, his tongue quick to take advantage as we discover each other, I can't resist the urge to run my hand through his soft curls. Passion doesn't have to be rough, and the slow kiss disarms me more than if he'd hurt me, and maybe in that quiet assault lies the treachery of his magic.

There's no fear or doubt—only peace. Peace for my lost life, my bitter heart, and all the parts of me I wished I could erase, especially the one that craves this.

The anger I felt when Arielle fed from me simmers under the surface, but it's not able to touch me, and I abandon myself to him.

He nibbles my ear lobe, his voice full of longing. "Do you want me to bite ye, Leo?"

My body tingles in anticipation. "Yes."

Long teeth pierce my jugular with skill, the painful sting quick to relent. The perfect blend of pain and self-loathing keeps me captive in Keenan's arms as he drinks from me with care, the hard planes of his chest pinning me to the wall.

My cells tingle as though I might condense into a cloud, and he hums against the slope of my neck before kissing the angle of my jaw. "I was right about ye. Ye're one of a kind." I taste my blood on his tongue as we kiss again, the metallic tang not as jarring as I expected, before he closes my useless hand around a small vial. "Drink this."

Mind dripping back into place, I uncork the small glass container and sniff the contents. "What is it?"

"A special sleep potion. It'll make ye look as good as dead, and I'll carry ye out of here without a care in the world." He brushes the sensitive spot behind my ear and bores his gaze into mine. "Don't worry, Leo. I will get ye back to yer princess."

With a quick tilt of my head, I gulp down the entire vial and tuck it inside my pockets not to leave any evidence behind. As my vision blurs, a halo appears over Keenan's head, and I pull him in for another soul-wrecking kiss before I lose consciousness.

## CHAPTER 3
# RAT RACE
### ALEC

Racing cars and egotistic vampires go hand in hand, making this McLaren the best *get-out-of-arranged-marriage-hell* free card I could have hoped for. The dark sky and the darker hills blur together as I speed to the city, a thick cover of clouds blanketing our escape.

I drum my fingers on my thighs, the wretched pants I took from Lucas Pereira one size too small, and risk a glance at the princess. Long, shiny strands of ebony hair have slipped from the hurried bun she tied at the nape of her neck, the red scarf around her neck contrasting with her white, smooth skin.

If it wasn't for the five armored cars tailing us, I'd pull over and kiss her bloody.

Almost on cue, her adrenaline-filled gaze travels from the passenger-side mirror to the back window. "They're still following us."

"Yes." With one hand on the steering wheel, I zoom through the outskirts of the city. "We need to ditch this flashy car as soon as we're downtown. A dozen Pereira guards are bound to keep up with my car-racing antics, and a hundred more will be canvassing the city before the night is over."

She shakes her head as though she's struggling to focus. "Where should we look for a boat?" she asks, apprehension thick in her tone.

Vampires secretly detest the sea. Not because we can't swim ten times as fast as a human, or hold our breaths underwater for hours. Not even because the salt wrecks the taste of blood. It's the fear of being stuck without food. Humans are scarce in the middle of an ocean, and the last thing any vampire wants to risk is dying of hunger.

My mouth dries up just thinking about it.

The high speed slams us into our seats as I accelerate again, heading toward the shore. "We're not going on a boat."

"But Lucas said—" She narrows her eyes, one arm braced across the car's door. "Where are we going then?"

"The angel told me where to go." I hesitate, searching for the right words. "You still trust Lucas, but I wouldn't be surprised if he's already spilled our entire conversation to his uncle. That kid has no spine."

A strangled snort pops out of her mouth. "Can't disagree with that."

"I'm going to drive close to the ocean, then we can kill the guards that managed to keep up, but we're actually going to switch cars and drive inland to Keenan's coordinates."

She shifts to face the rear of the car and brushes my arm. "How many of them are there? Five SUVs with one to three soldiers inside each of them?"

My gaze flicks to the rearview mirror. "I'll lose a couple before we stop, but don't worry, I can take them."

She sinks back into the passenger seat, her perfect brow arched in defiance. "And leave me with nothing to do?"

"You don't know how to fight."

Her jaw opens. "You refused to teach me."

"You only asked *yesterday*." I add, unable to bite back a grin at how cute she looks when she's outraged.

Long black nails skim my stomach down to my crotch, her light touch distracting as hell. "You taught me a thing or two yesterday..."

A full-on smile stretches my lips, and my eyes dart to hers. I'm simply caught by the undertow of her ocean-blue stare and the barely-veiled joy brimming from her humorous quip. *Fuck, I love this.*

But I can't forget what really happened tonight. She became Queen, and I'm the one tasked to protect her. I might not agree with everything the crown has asked me to do over the years, or even understand the pressure that comes with ruling over an entire continent, but I know she'll be as good a monarch as her mother. The Shadow World will be better off with her as Queen than it was with Victor as King.

Arielle Delacroix needs to sit on the throne of shadows and claim her rightful place in the world, and it's on me to get her there. How bad is it that all I want to do right now is make her mine again?

It's like my body is cursed now that it knows what it's missing, but I resist the urge to pull her in for an irresponsible kiss. "We'll be long gone by the time the next batch comes, but I'll leave you one. If you insist."

"How generous of you."

She has no training, but she's a newborn vampire. She can do enough damage to kill one or two while I get rid of the others.

I pass her one of the slim, aconite blades I slipped in Lucas' jacket before we left. "Here. Stake them through the heart with that, and they'll be easy to finish."

"Alright." She grips the hilt of the dagger and runs her index finger across the blade with an expression of quiet wonderment.

The buildings around us grow taller and taller as we make our way downhill to the heart of the city. I ignore the red lights and zip past the stop signs, counting on my lightning reflexes to avoid an accident. Pereira's guards nip our wheels, ready to pounce if the opportunity arises. A tight corner comes up ahead, so I grip the steering wheel and take the curve a little wide to open up my exit, a technique that allows me to go full-throttle sooner and head into the next straight line faster.

Powerful honks rebel in my wake, the traffic disturbed by the race. I repeat the feat until the dark expanse of the ocean flashes between the high rise towers. Once I'm satisfied that we lost a couple of SUVs, I slam the breaks and pop the door open. I run to the curb where Arielle is already waiting and guide her into an alleyway to force the guards to get out of their car and follow us on foot.

A handful of them run up on our rear, gunshots tearing through the air. We run past the building's corner and climb up the gutters on each side of the back alley.

I'd overestimated the guards' ability to think on their feet, and they barrel past our hiding spot without hesitation—as though we're little girls running from the big bad wolf. It's too easy to jump on the back of the leader to stake him through the heart. I use my gun to incapacitate another while I behead the third.

Arielle sticks her blade inside the fourth man's back, a little too high to kill. The vamp propels her over his shoulder and pauses, probably torn between his survival instincts and the need to complete his mission. The king certainly didn't give these half wits permission to strike his betrothed down, and I take advantage of his hesitation to slit his throat.

The fifth member of the team manages to lodge a bullet in my neck, but Arielle  stakes him clean through the heart, and he vanishes in a cloud of dust.

"Are you alright?" she asks, the thrill of the hunt coloring her cheeks.

I cough up a mouthful of blood, the wound on my neck already healing as I scan the street for our next ride. "Yes."

A motorcycle and its owner are waiting for traffic to clear on the road up ahead.

"Perfect." I grip the leather coat of the motorcyclist and sink my fangs into the poor man's neck. I haven't fed at all today, and I need enough energy to heal better and see us through this. Blood sprays to the roof of my mouth, not quenching half my hunger, but I still stop right before killing him and snap off the strap of his helmet. The man's limp body slumps to the pavement as I straddle the motorcycle and hand Arielle the helmet, my dick already half-hard at the sight of her freckled with ashes and blood.

She doesn't actually need a helmet. Our bodies are meant to heal from pretty much anything but a stake through the heart and a severed head, but we'll blend in better this way.

Arielle pushes the helmet down on her head, hops on behind me, and snakes her arms around my midriff. An unwanted rush of adrenaline rakes through me, and I'm suddenly more nervous about this operation than my last ten combined, the usual calm and clarity I get whenever I do what I do best erased by the simplicity of her touch. This isn't just another mission.

Her sweet, honeyed scent holds me captive, her full breasts pressed tightly to my back. The black dress rode up her creamy thighs when she straddled the bike, and I can't resist the urge to squeeze her bare knee, wishing I had all the time in the world to imprint the sight of her on a motorcycle—and her damn sexy stilettos—to memory.

"Drive us out of here, Mr. Beaumont," she murmurs in my ear, her sultry voice filling me with pride and desire.

# CHAPTER 4
# A VICIOUS SNARE
## ALEC

The queen of the Delacroix empire sneaks her small hand up my thigh with confidence as I drive into traffic, inching dangerously close to my crotch. "Mmm... You weren't kidding when you said violence makes you horny."

The wicked games she plays with her hand might just have us crash into a wall if she's not careful, the tight pants more than uncomfortable.

"Stop it," I say with a hint of regret.

With a giggle, she finally stops teasing me and flattens both palms to my chest, the pain in my groin slow to relent.

The motorcycle is more malleable and can squeeze into narrow alleys, attracting way less attention and allowing me to weave through the city efficiently while keeping a low profile. I whip around a few tight corners to make good time, but with enough respect for the traffic signals not to alarm anyone.

"The hangar Keenan told me about back at the estate is on the opposite side of town," I say.

"Do you think he's planning to double-cross us?"

I take a moment before I answer. Keenan was hired by the king to do a job, and if he always flaked out on his contracts, he wouldn't be one of the most renowned sword-for-hire in the Shadow World.

But I've heard enough about him to know that he's got a code of honor, and that angels are a dying species, their kind quickly dwindling in numbers.

"Whatever payment he hoped to get from Pereira, we can offer ten times more now, and I believe his genuine interest in Leo."

"I do, too." She squeezes me tighter, her embrace somehow more intimate than it was last night. Yesterday, there was a...distance between us. We were enjoying our first and last night together, our *only* night.

The way she holds on to me now leaves me no doubt that there will be others. Feeling like I'm riding on a cloud, I park the motorcycle a few blocks from the given address and check the exact location with my phone.

A throng of missed calls from Sebastian and a myriad of angry, worried texts clutter the screen, and I roll my eyes as I turn the screen to Arielle.

She huffs at his language. "Thousands of kilometers away, he still thinks the world revolves around him."

A short text from an unknown number stands out among the angry notifications.

ETA 30 minutes. 546945.

I don't respond, thinking that if Keenan got my number, he doesn't expect me to reply, and that if it's anyone else, I don't want to give them an incentive to track my phone. I cut off the signal and tuck it back into my pocket, itching to get out of the clothes I borrowed.

I canvas the streets and find nothing out of place. "We should walk the rest of the way on foot, to be more discrete."

The lights are dim and few and far between in this part of town, and graffiti peppers the buildings with Portuguese slang and crude imagery. I shoot a glance to the roof of the adjacent building. "We can get a better view from up there."

We climb the wall to the first balcony and use the rust-flecked emergency ladder to reach the flat roof. Once there, I check the block below, but the only sounds audible are distant sirens and the rumble of the air-conditioning units crammed in the windows. Vapors of industrial solvent float through the seedy neighborhood.

"We're good for now," I announce.

My palms are still sweaty from the motorcycle ride, my hard dick aching from the way her thighs squeezed mine. "We should approach the address Keenan gave me and watch it from a dist—"

Arielle glides a finger below the lapel of my jacket. "Remember when I promised to have you fired?"

A wolfish grin blooms on my lips, my hands instinctively flying to her waist. "How could I forget such a lovely threat."

"Since I'm now your boss, I'm willing to break that promise. Depends on how well you follow orders."

Her luminous smile makes my dick throb, and I pull her in for a wild, dizzying kiss. Her ruby-red lips are sweeter than I remembered, her hungry hands sneaking under the hem of my shirt like she wants to tear my clothes off. Adrenaline boils in my blood and heightens my senses to the point where pleasure and pain blur. Jesus, I should put a halt to this now before it goes too far. Before I completely fall for her and lose what small part of my brain I have left.

This is serious shit. I should pull back and re-draw the line between us. Stealing the princess' V-card before a sham marriage is one thing, but fooling around with the queen is another.

And fuck, it's hot. I want a second night with her. And a third. I don't care how dangerous it is. I don't care that she'll probably break my heart.

She looks me up and down, her tousled hair and red lips stealing my breath. "Drop your pants, Mr. Beaumont."

"Your wish is my command, Your Highness."

She wrangles her white, virginal panties past the kink in her knees, the hiked-up skirt of her black dress revealing a blue garter at her mid-thigh. Saliva dries from my mouth, the sight of the ritualistic apparel twisting my insides. This was supposed to be her wedding night, and the thought of ravishing her on a roof and making her scream *my name* instead suddenly becomes my new life goal.

I fumble with the belt, pull my pants down, and capture her in my arms. Without missing a beat, she wraps her thighs around my midriff, the potent scent of her arousal driving me wild. It's hurried and messy, but after last night, it feels only too easy and natural to pin her to the rooftop enclosure's wall.

She sinks her nails into my shoulder blade and wrenches me closer. "Don't hold back," she pants. "I need you."

"Oh, Lucky." I kiss her neck, euphoria flowing thick in my veins, and I don't remember the last time I was so hard, my dick reacting to her touch like I'm a fucking teenager.

I bury myself deep inside her, and she goes mad for it, her head falling to the red brick wall at her back as I hold her weight with one hand. Slurred words of encouragement ghost along the shell of my ear as I flatten my free palm to the red brick to give her a moment, dying to thrust hard and fast, my blood racing with each breath.

"Wait. The necklace," she whimpers.

I check if the wretched thing got tangled in her hair, but the metal is actually burning-hot.

She slides to her feet, her eyes wide with fear. "It burns."

The hot links blister her neck, and the scent of burnt flesh pervades the air. Red and black flakes of skin peel off and curl at the heat. Dark red blood pools in the fresh burns to heal them, but the process only manages to keep her alive, not stop the necklace from burning hotter and hotter. My gaze darts across the roof like a drunken bee, my mind reeling for an explanation. I concentrate on my senses, but not one heartbeat is audible in the distance, and my killer instincts tell me we're completely alone.

A primal desperation kicks in, and I grip both sides of the chain to tear it from her neck. The links singe my hands, but I push through the pain, the necklace resistant to my assaults. A sickening squeeze tightens my gut as it starts to glow under my frozen stare, and I jolt away.

Red tears pour out of her eyes. "What's happening?"

I grip my hair, my chest threatening to implode from helplessness. "I don't know."

The red-orange links flicker in the night.

"It's...better." She pats down her burned chest. "I think it's you... it gets hotter whenever you touch me."

A chill numbs my arms and legs. "Fuck! It started burning when I entered you...it's a fidelity collar."

We exchange a long look, my hands shaking with rage.

Her long vampire teeth flash into view as she wrestles the fiery necklace in vain. "I swear to you, Alec. If I survive this, I'm going to kill the damned bastard."

# CHAPTER 5
# SCARLET WITCH
## ARIELLE

Burns feel ten times worse to a vampire. We run colder than humans, so nothing prepared me for the white-hot pain of being set ablaze. The chain ensnares my neck, still hot enough to hurt, but slightly cooler since Alec took a giant leap away from me.

The vampire's edges tremble like it pains him to keep his distance when I'm in distress.

I wrap a hand around my throat, the fire dying down to ashes. "I can't breathe. It's like... I'm—"

Vampires don't need air to live, but they do need it to speak, and the last words die on my tongue. If I was mortal, I'd be dead by asphyxiation. My throat bobs, my body slowly adjusting to the lack of oxygen, and a sluggish ache takes hold of my muscles.

I prepare myself for the worst, thinking I might die right here, but the spell seems to have run its course, and I motion to my throat to make him understand I'm mute.

My bodyguard breathes heavily, his hair in disarray, his belt buckle still undone, his professional facade in shambles. "You can't breathe anymore."

I give Alec a tensed nod.

He steps closer, but I recoil, terrified that the spell will activate again.

He spins on his heels, chin angled to the sky. "Fuck. Fuck. Fuck."

Remaining at a safe distance, he guides me from roof to roof until we reach the address Keenan gave us. Sleek black asphalt reflects the moonlight behind the industrial hangar, the long runway allowing for enough space to take off and land. Alec feeds the right code to the keypad next to the front door and holds the door for me as I slip inside, being careful not to brush against him. The deserted hangar holds a small jet.

Alec checks his phone. "They should be here soon."

As if on cue, the garage door whines on its hinges and slowly rises into the air. An electric-blue Mercedes drives in, the door quickly lowering behind it as Keenan parks next to us.

The sight of Leo lying unconscious in the passenger seat stokes the panic in my veins. I run to his side, concentrating on the faint thump of his sluggish heartbeats. *He's alive.* The blood tainting my first-blood's neck makes my beast roar in jealousy, and I grip the edge of the rolled-down window hard enough to crack it.

"Now, don't bite. I pretended to kill him, and it had to look believable," Keenan says quickly.

Unable to speak, I run my fingers through Leo's soft hair and brush it away from his closed lids.

"Don't worry, he'll wake up in a few hours." The angel slams the door closed behind and freezes, eyes fixed on my neck. "Fuck... It's active?"

"Yes," Alec whispers, his face still white as a sheet.

The angel dashes toward me and extends his fingers to the snare around my neck. "They're probably tracking us with it. How long has it been orange like that? We have to get if off."

Alec grips his arm, stopping the angel just as he's about to poke at the collar. "Ten minutes at most. I tried to tear it off again, but it only angered whatever spell it contains. The more I touch it—or her —the more it burns."

The angel pouts like he swallowed a mouthful of ashes. "A fidelity collar?"

Alec gives a sharp nod. "I think so. Can you break it?"

Keenan squints at the chained necklace, his thick brows furrowed. "Nae. This isn't a rookie enchantment, and I'm no warlock." He tilts his head to the side, his eyes lost in contemplation for a moment. "But I know someone that might be able to help."

"Might?" Alec barks darkly, his patience running thin.

"Let me think on it for a minute." Keenan holds one hand in front of him, signalling for us to wait. "First things first, we have to take off before they track us here." He walks to the other side of the car, cradles Leo's body in his arms, and ushers us into the plane.

The private jet has two seats out front for the pilot and co-pilot and three rows of two spacious seats in the back. It's half the size of the one we travelled to Brazil with, but it'll do nicely.

Keenan deposits Leo in a front row seat and secures his seatbelt. The small *click* resonates across the hull before he meets my inquisitive gaze. "Yes. I think my witch friend would help us with this, but witches are skittish, and her demon is ten times worse." Without another word of explanation, he heads directly for the cockpit, bending down not to bump his head on the cockpit's door frame.

I sit in the seat across the aisle from Leo and grip the armrests. The pain in my neck has sparked a humongous headache between my eyes, and my frustration at not being able to speak makes the situation ten times worse. A witch... I swallow hard at the thought. I've never even met one aside from the handful of warlocks that have been working for my family for generations, and they're not allowed to socialize with us, or us with them.

Witches and demons... don't mix.

Alec seals the airplane door. "You know a witch powerful enough to undo this? How?"

Keenan plops a pair of headphones over his ears and opens the back hangar door with the press of a button. "There are hundreds of them, Beaumont. You just have to know where to look."

"Covens are too dangerous—"

Keenan interrupts him. "No coven, just her. I promise. One witch. She owes me a favor."

"And where is this witch of yours?" Alec asks, suspicion thick in his voice.

The plane slowly wobbles out onto the runway as Kennan maneuvers the controls with the ease of someone who's flown a hundred flights. "Virginia."

THE HOURS TRICKLE down slowly until I pass out from exhaustion. The necklace cools down over the span of the trip, but my healing powers struggle to repair the damage already done. The sum of it leaves me in tatters, my muscles aching all over.

Keenan nudges me awake before we descend, and I smooth down my hair, trying hard to ignore the red blisters on my neck. Alec sulks in the corner, his face angled to the side like he can't bear to look at me, and Leo's still out cold.

The landing goes by without a hitch, and before I can totally chase off the haze of sleep, Keenan opens the door to greet his witch friend, a slender woman with a mane of loose, strawberry blonde curls.

"Hey, beautiful girl." Keenan's eyes soften as he makes way for her. "Glad you could make it." The angel is an outrageous flirt, but I get the impression that this woman is significant to him.

She grins in response and strolls past the angel and into the small airplane. A tall, delicious-looking blond human wearing jeans and a navy blue t-shirt trails behind her, a black satchel hanging from his grasp.

The witch checks her watch. "How long do we have before they find us?"

Keenan's lips curl down. "No more than twenty minutes."

The woman's blonde companion inspects the hangar. "And what kind of company are we expecting?"

Alec clears his throat, his arms braced over his chest. "I'd say twenty. Half of them green, and maybe a handful of elite soldiers," he says in his matter-of-fact, professional drawl.

A tired smile tugs at one corner of the witch's mouth. "Just twenty, eh?"

Keenan closes the door behind them. "Hey, I didn't say it'd be an easy favor. Where's Grumpy?"

"Out of town, but we can manage," the human answers with a pout.

Keenan chuckles under his breath, his blues eyes dancing at some inside joke between them. "I'm sure you can, Thomas."

"This is Arielle Delacroix, heir to the throne," Alec announces ceremoniously, skipping all pleasantries.

I stand up straight, but the witch is taller than me by a few inches.

She tilts her head to the side and holds out her hand in greeting. Discreet tattoos mark her as possessed by a demon-—one snakes around her finger while another dips between the swell of her breasts. "I'm Alana, and this is Thom. I want to help, but I also haven't heard good things about your family."

"What's your price, then?"Alec asks carefully, his measured tone cracking at the end.

The witch doesn't turn to him, her intent gaze set on me. "You will answer my questions honestly about your court's witches and warlocks, and on top of that, you will owe me a favor."

The bright aura around her shines with power, the scent of her vanilla and strawberries blood so potent that my mouth fills with saliva as I shake her outstretched hand.

Witch's blood is the ultimate delicacy for demons, the strength and stamina brought on by a few drops making an encounter like this incredibly rare. Only the reigning monarch is allowed to taste the blood of the few warlocks and witches owned by our family, the use of black-market blood strictly outlawed by my kin, as withdrawal can send even the best of us into a killing frenzy.

A demon-witch alliance is almost unheard of, their covens bent on killing as many demons as they possibly can, but if this one is owned by one of us...

Alec seems to be following the same train of thought. "Shouldn't we discuss this with your demon?"

Alana's mouth opens on a sarcastic smile, her jaw slightly askew. "*My* demon doesn't own me. These"—she holds her hand over the snake tattoo on her chest— "are not what they seem. Can I come closer?"

"Are you sure about this, Lana?" her companion asks.

"I am." She inches closer, her green eyes wide. "*She looks so young...*" she thinks, her previously impassive stare betraying a hint of empathy and surprise.

I concentrate hard on the flavor of her inner voice and try to answer telepathically, but the words get...stuck, not projected as they should be. I should really have asked Alec to teach me telepathy before this.

Her gaze falls to the smoldering chain around my neck. "Keenan said your fiancé put a slave-binding spell in a piece of jewelry?"

With a nod, I wrangle the neckline of my dress away from the metal links of the cursed necklace.

A snarl curls her lips. "No one should ever be put through that." She raises her hands in front of her and meets my gaze. "Can I touch it?"

Pressing my lips together, I brace myself for the pain. Alana inspects the links one by one, handling them as delicately as she can, but I still wince as she works the links away from my burnt flesh, her fingers soon tainted with blood—and a hint of melted skin.

"Can you dust it?" Thomas asks expectantly.

Alana shakes her head. "No. It's a very well-crafted spell."

Thomas gets a leather-bound book out of her bag and leafs through it. "I've heard of these bindings, where the spell is bound to an object instead of a person. It's incredibly rare, and it usually requires the subject of the spell to make an unbreakable vow."

Keenan scratches the back of his neck, his brows pulled in a guilty frown. "I think the wedding vows were meant to act as the promise of fidelity."

Alana's gaze snaps up to the angel. "What set it off, then, if the wedding didn't happen?"

Heat pools in my chest as I remember what Alec and I were doing when the damn magical snare burned up.

My bodyguard clenches his fists, looking almost ashen. "We were... We tried to have sex."

Keenan curses loudly, his accent thick with annoyance. "Mbrise an diabhal do chnámha. Couldn't wait to get your dick wet, Beaumont?"

"We didn't know it'd set it off," Alec grits through his teeth.

"It's probably enchanted to keep you obedient *and* faithful, but only the second part is already active." Alana's nose wrinkles as she grazes the deep burns on my chest once more. "You've got better healing capabilities than the others of your kind I've met, but these are getting worse." Her piercing green eyes meet mine with determination and pity. "I can break the spell, but I'm not going to lie, you might not survive it. Normally, I'd delay the procedure to do some research, but you're clearly out of time."

Alec raises a hand between us. "Wait a min—"

I press my finger over his mouth and meet his gaze head-on, commanding his attention. "*I trust her.*"

His pupils dilate, the gold ring around his irises so thin his eyes are almost all red. "*Are you sure?*"

He heard me! The joy of success is quickly chased away by the reality of my situation. I won't become a mindless slave to a man I despise, and I convey that with a grave nod as I catch Alana's gaze again. *"Do what you have to do."*

She eyes Alec and Keenan in turn. "This might get bloody. Do I have to worry about one of you trying to eat me while I do this? If so, you should probably get out of the plane *now*."

Both demons swallow hard but shake their heads in the negative, and Alec moves to wrap a protective arm around my waist before he jerks backward at the last second. "Hell... I'm not leaving her."

Alana's companion hands her the black bag. She unzips the flap and starts unpacking a wide array of spell materials, vials, and minerals on the nearby table before she passes a long rope to Alec. "Tie your queen up in the seat here." She motions for the seat behind me, in the middle row of the plane.

Alec's fist tightens over the rope. "How tight should the knots be?"

The green-eyed witch squints at my lover as though she's sizing up his determination. "As tight as she can bear. We've only got one shot at this."

# CHAPTER 6

# HUMAN

## LEO

The bitter scent of incense, charcoal, and burnt flesh coaxes me from a dreamless slumber, and I sit up, startled. The princess is tied to a plane seat, her arms bound behind her back and her feet tied down. Alec glowers behind her, his expression unreadable as a woman with red hair murmurs a litany under her breath.

"What the—"

Alec kills the rest of my question with a lethal look, and his reaction calms my initial fight-or-flight instinct, keeping me from jumping out of my seat at the sight of her bound and helpless.

Smoke rises up from a light brazier, the copper bowl holding the flames as thick as my thumb. The wretched necklace Felipe Pereira gave to Arielle glows bright-orange around her neck, and whatever magic is inside it is hurting her.

"What's going on?" I croak, my voice dry and choppy. The aftertaste of jasmine tingles along the roof of my mouth.

A blond man with bright blue eyes inches toward me with a finger pressed to his lips. "We're almost done with the ritual, Leo, we just need a few more minutes," he whispers softly.

The red blisters peppering Arielle's neck dry up my tongue, my mind reeling, and I try to stand, but I'm strapped in with a seatbelt. My knuckles turn white against the cushioned armrests.

"Take it easy. Keenan fed you a sleeping potion," the man says, his blue eyes almost as blue as Keenan's.

A furious blush heats my cheeks at the memory of the angel's kiss, but I rub down my face and shake the unwanted thoughts out of my mind, concentrating on the current crisis instead.

Alec's jaw ticks as the woman kneeling in front of Arielle presses the end of an incense stick to one of the chain links. Arielle writhes in her restraints, her long fangs out like she's desperate to tear through the woman's neck.

Blood drains from my face, the severity of the situation hitting me square in the face. "Is she going to be okay?"

"She should be. Lana knows what she's doing. The necklace had a few tricky safeguards added to it, but your friend is stronger than most. If she wasn't so quick to heal herself and contain the worst of the necklace's magic, she'd already be dead." He speaks with confidence, his voice measured and calm.

I squint, observing his curly blond hair and blue eyes, wondering if he's an angel, too. "Who are you?"

He extends his hand. "Thom Walker. Nice to meet you."

"Leo."

Thom crouches next to me—at a perfectly polite distance—and leans in to continue our quiet conversation. "They told me you were human. How did you end up in this mess, if you don't mind me asking?"

The skin of my cheek tingles as though I've been slapped in the face. I bet he's only making conversation to distract me from whatever they have to do to help Arielle. I know that, and yet I sit stock-still next to the weirdly familiar stranger. "I'm her first-blood."

His eyes narrow, a terrible cloud passing over his previously calm features. "You're a blood slave?"

"I—Yeah." A vicious shiver rocks through me as I hide my face in my palms. There's no if or buts about it. I might have technically signed up for this, but I'm a slave, and it feels both good and wretched to hear it out loud and have it acknowledged by someone else, when everybody on the island and at the castle were so quick to brush over that simple fact.

Thom shoots Alec a nasty glance over his shoulder and inches closer. "Do you want out, Leo?"

I consider him for a long minute before I answer, "I don't know. Who's asking?"

"Just me. I'm human, too."

I eye him up and down again, not sure he's telling the truth. "And how did *you* end up here?"

"It's the family business." His gaze drops like a stone, but quickly rises up again. "You say the word, and I'll make sure you leave with us today."

He's offering me freedom like it's candy, and it boils my blood. "It's not that easy."

His brows furrow. "Should we be worried? Are they going to turn on us?"

"No, but it doesn't mean—" I pause, searching for the right words. This man is a perfect stranger, and I don't have to justify myself to him, but somehow, I feel like I do. "I'm not a blood slave in the way you implied. It's complicated, okay?"

He nods slowly and slides back into his seat across the aisle. "Let me know if you change your mind."

The witch continues to work on the necklace, every new step causing Arielle to writhe harder and harder until a gray tint glazes over the skin of her arms, chest, and face. Charred flesh flakes off her burned neck and harsh shivers quake through her. Even when she was covered in Alec's blood or crying over her arranged marriage, she never lost herself. The spark in her eyes is gone now, snuffed out by the pain, and I click off the seatbelt, ready to put a stop to this.

The sight of her so vulnerable and broken... I want to burn down the ones responsible.

"Fuck. Stop!" Alec echoes my sentiment as he punches the head-rest of the empty seat behind him. "She's too weak."

"I'm almost done," the witch shouts, holding a hand up to the revved-up bodyguard to calm him down. The tips of her fingers have blistered so deep that blood trickles down her palm.

Arielle follows the liquid running down the woman's hands like she wants to lap it off, her restraints preventing her from eating the woman whole.

"Who is she?" I ask Thom, my heart beating faster in my chest as Arielle thrashes harder from side to side. "What is she doing?"

"She's trying to save her," he repeats patiently.

"She's killing her!" I jump out of my seat, but Thom wraps his arms around me like a vice, holding me back. He's not as strong as a vampire, but the world around me blurs, the haze of the sleeping potion still thick in my veins.

An unbidden scream tears through Arielle's throat as the links of the chain give with a high-pitched *tink*. Her body slumps on the seat like a puppet liberated from its strings, and her chest rises and falls for the first time since I woke up. A chill slams through me at the realization that all that time, she couldn't breathe.

The witch chokes on a sniffle and rises to her feet, her bottom lip tucked between her teeth, her wounded hands held close to her chest. "She needs blood. Now!"

Thom releases me, and I elbow my way past Keenan to reach Arielle. Alec switches places with me, allowing me to stand behind her and offer her my wrist while my other hand holds the headrest of her seat for balance.

Long dark hair cascades down her back as her head wobbles from side to side, her lids drooping like she's about to pass out. A heart-wrenching mix of soot, blood, and melted skin sticks to the dark waves.

"Shh. You're okay now." My heart stumbles as I press my wrist deeper inside her mouth. "Drink."

*I need her to be okay. I need her to be okay. I needhertobeokay.*

36

The tension in my spine eases when Arielle gulps the blood hungrily, and I smooth down her hair with a shaky hand. *That was too close.*

Alec bends in front of her and kisses her knuckles. My eyes flick to each of the others in turn, still trying to catch up. Keenan blinked out of the plane, his broad frame nowhere to be found in the cramped space.

The witch grazes the swirly tattoo evident in her cleavage before she starts stowing her equipment back inside her bag, the vicious burns on her hands somehow healed.

Thom wraps an arm around his friends' shoulders and pecks the side of her head. "You saved her, Lana."

I glance down to Arielle, the princess still drinking from me like I'm the last oasis in the universe, the pain in my wrist numbed by either the adrenaline or the remnants of the sleeping potion. She's not a predator now. She *needs* me, and I whisper words of encouragement in her ear, desperate to take her pain away.

I catch Thom staring at us, and his piercing blue gaze softens as it travels between Arielle and me. Nervous of his scrutiny, I angle my back to him to shield Arielle from view and create a bubble to give her privacy as she feeds.

Like I said. It's complicated.

# CHAPTER 7
# ABEL
## ALEC

The broken pieces of the cursed necklace crunch under Arielle's heels, her lips pursed in disgust as she breathes in and out. A hint of life slowly returns to her cheeks from all the blood she just ingested, and Leo slumps in the seat behind her, his heartbeats slightly uneven.

The burns around her neck are still deep and red, and I slice off the rope holding her legs, my jaw clenched. "I can't believe I was stupid enough to set off that necklace..."

"You didn't know," she says patiently, a layer of ashes and cinder flaking off her neck.

*I can't forgive myself for being so sloppy, I just can't. I need to focus on her safety and nothing else. Besides, I'm not the guy for her. I could never be King* "You almost died."

"I didn't."

"Still—" Our gazes cross, and I get the feeling that she's just read my thoughts, her vulnerable gaze full of tenderness and fear. "Are you reading my mind right now?"

"Kiss me," she slurs sheepishly, clearly a little groggy from the ritual—or the leftover sleep potion in Leo's blood. Her hand shoots out to grab my tie, but I quickly jolt away from her grasp.

*Holy shit! Did she hear me overthinking the possibility of ever becoming King? Jesus... I don't want to be King, and we only spent one night together. Does she think that I expect her to commit to me like that because we slept together? Or did she just catch the part about me not being the guy for her?*

*Fuck. Fuck. Fuck.*

Despite the urge to wrap myself around her, I keep my distance, suddenly fearing her incredible abilities. I don't want to second-guess my thoughts around her or feel self-conscious of my inner musings, but how can I not?

"I'm supposed to protect you, not almost kill you with my care-lessness." I need to think more with my brain and less with the part of my anatomy that is just obsessed with the feel of her... Jesus, even now, weak and whiplashed as she looks, all I can think about is leading her away from these men and holding her close.

"Hey, lovebirds. Enough bickering. We have company," Keenan says, his deep celt accent intruding on our *argument*. The angel grabs a saber at the back of the plane and holds one out for me.

I close my eyes and concentrate on my senses, caging in the Arielle-focussed beast that howls in my bloodstream. Rain drums along the white tarp covering the hangar. The large dome storage unit serves as cover in the middle of the field, the building located at the end of the long stretch of asphalt we used for landing. It's a dead-end road in the middle of nowhere, and I can hear tires screeching from a mile away. "Keenan's right. We have company."

Arielle moves to stand, but her legs wobble. "I wish I could stake a dozen of them, but I feel like I'm going to pass out any minute."

Leo looks about ready to do the same, his eyes glossy and narrow like he's still half-asleep.

"You're in no shape to fight." Without meaning to, I peck her forehead and pass my gun to the human, Thom. "Stay with them."

He clicks the safety off with a curt nod, and I catch a glimpse of his witch friend, Alana, as she stows what looks to be a syringe back into her bag. Shaking off the urge to ask her what she just did, I take the sword from Keenan and test its grip. It's lightweight and malleable, so it'll do nicely.

Alana ties a utility belt around her hips and pulls a short-bladed dagger from her bag.

I fight off the urge to frown. What the hell does she think she's doing? "You won't do much damage with that. You should stay in the plane."

She tosses me a half-playful, half-annoyed look. "Don't worry about me. I have my ways."

The mouth-watering scent of her blood taints the air as we filter out of the plane, and I raise a questioning brow at Keenan. This isn't a game or an opportunity to show off some flashy, dark mojo, especially if she juiced up on something.

I lean closer to the angel. "If the girl can hold her own in a street fight, good for her, but we should err on the side of caution. She's a witch, not a ninja." I won't let any sense of pride or misplaced showmanship get in the way of Arielle's safety. "I won't risk myself to save your friend if she gets a pair of fangs to the neck."

Keenan waves my concerns away. "Don't underestimate the witch, Beaumont. She's got moves the likes of which you've never seen."

My jaw ticks at the playfulness of his voice. "In my line of work, there's not much I haven't seen."

"Then you'll be pleasantly surprised!" the witch shouts over her shoulder as five SUVs roll under the hangar roof.

Smoke rises from their wheels as they come to a sudden halt, and enemy soldiers filter out of the black cars. If we were humans, a grenade or a bazooka would be enough to wipe us all out, but immortals are made of sturdier stuff. Since we can heal from most... explosive wounds, the fastest way to kill a demon is up close and personal.

I count as twelve men hit the pavement, a handful of them still waiting in the cars. They're not all vampires, but an eclectic blend of demons, and my throat tightens. Twenty Pereiras, I could handle. The Pereira army relies on numbers instead of brains, but these thugs could be anything from angels to shadow walkers, and highly unpredictable in both strength and powers, which puts them at an enormous advantage. I canvas our attackers for their leader, knowing one of them must be in charge.

A familiar silhouette slides out of the armored SUV closest to me, and I choke on a tight breath.

Jasper.

My brother.

The god-damned head of the royal guard—and my boss.

*What the fuck.*

I hold out an arm to gain Keenan's and Alana's attention. "Wait!"

Jasper strolls in front of his men without a care in the world, his hands buried in his sleek black jacket. "You managed to escape Brazil. Impressive."

My brows are stuck together in question, but my voice is steady as I declare, "Our queen needs to get home, where she belongs."

Jasper flashes me his teeth, the smile devoid of any warmth. "With her gone, the Delacroix are done."

Any leftover hope that I'd misunderstood the situation shrivels in my chest. He's not here to help. Jesus...my own brother is trying to overthrow the Delacroix empire, and I didn't even see it coming.

*By Nyx, I've been played since the beginning... his unexpected jump in the ranks, the weird-ass decisions, the nonsensical changes he made to the royal guard...*

I thought his big ego had pushed him to assert his authority over us. I thought he wanted to get revenge on me for outshining me. I thought it was all about him, like always, but clearly, he'd been moving pieces on the chess board for a bigger scheme.

A heavy weight settles in my chest. "You orchestrated the whole thing. You sent me away so you could get rid of Victor."

"Victor was killed by the Zhaos," he says, far too pleased with himself.

It makes sense... Ludovic Delacroix, Arielle's older brother, was feared and respected. He had that mystical quality about him, an affinity for darkness that seemed bigger than life. He could hold the attention of a room with one breath, whereas Victor was always considered to be a pushover. Still... I'd thought that my dumbass brothers would position themselves to manipulate him, not get rid of him altogether.

*I'm still missing something. They killed Victor because he was in the way, but my brothers don't have the necessary pedigree to hold a crown.*

"People who steal crowns only warm it up until the next rebellion. Without the Delacroix, it'll be chaos in Europe," I say slowly, gauging his reaction.

I need to keep him talking, so I can finish the puzzle.

He shakes his head at my pessimist view of his rebellion. "No chaos. Adele will rule until her oldest kid comes of age."

Suddenly, it clicks. I think back to that night in the garden when my older brother was cozied up to the queen consort's first-blood. If Garrett wants to steal the throne, he needs a blue-blooded wife. Who could be better than the current queen consort, the daughter of the most affluent Prime Minister in centuries? That's the *only* way a Beaumont could hope to retain power.

My brothers killed Victor so Garrett could marry Adele Chastain.

A dry snicker cracks from my throat, because it's laughable. "Garrett and Adele on the throne together? You've all gone mad. Arielle isn't going to abdicate. Now, little brother, you go home. You go and tell them that the rightful heir to the throne is alive and well because they will rally around her no matter what."

Contempt twists his lips in an ugly grimace. "Now, who's gone mad?"

I'm only halfway done unraveling his plans. He's here, and not the Pereiras, which means—

My muscles coil, and my grip tightens around the hilt of the saber. This was a carefully planned operation, and the princess is a loose end. "You tracked the necklace...*you're* the one who had it made."

He nods the way only a cartoon villain can, with enough arrogance to melt my brain. "And I gave it to Pereira as an early wedding gift. I thought I could spare her life this way, but you had to break her out before the wedding. Come on now, brother. It's ten to one."

Jasper couldn't hope to kill the princess with Delacroix-trained soldiers that are loyal to the crown, so he hired mercenaries. He's not here to chat, or negotiate, or figure out a way to better his position. He's simply here to get rid of her once and for all.

He glances at my allies, sizing them up. "You've got what? A pretty bird and a little girl? Don't throw your life away like that. Surrender the princess, and the three of us can finally get what we deserve."

*I can't believe this...*

After years of idle threats, I finally have to do it for real. I'm going to kill my brother.

Before I can move, his men attack, and my instincts kick into gear. I raise my sword to block an incoming large projectile, and the potent scent of it assaults my nose. They knew they were not going to get anywhere with guns, so they brought aconite-laced bolts. Smart.

I'm the best assassin the night court has ever seen because, ever since I was a newborn vampire, I could split my brain into two parts. While one side of my brain avoids the bolts, daggers, and swords coming for my head, the other side evaluates the battlefield with stone-cold accuracy.

8 vampires with hand-to-hand weapons.

6 snipers.

3 unknowns.

And Jasper, but the coward quickly takes cover in his vehicle, the tinted glass erasing him from view.

The bitter tang of an aconite bomb takes out half the snipers, blasting them to the ground, and the witch dashes into the fray.

Keenan already blinked behind the others, stopping the onslaught of bolts and allowing us to take on the wave of hand-to-hand attackers. Despite what I said, I keep an eye on the witch, feeling indebted to her for saving Arielle. She dashes into action, moving faster than I expected her to—faster than any human should.

I stake a vampire clean through his heart and behead him only for three of the unknowns to use the opportunity to encircle me, their swords on the offensive. They're fast, faster than most vampires, but not faster than me. I twirl the blade of my saber around and parry their blows, keeping them at bay while I figure out what I'm dealing with. Deep cracks run in their skin, the mark of a human shape-shifter. The full moon must be tonight, the creatures ready to shed their current skin in favor of another.

That'll work in our favor. The suckers can basically survive any wound, including decapitation, but they become weaker around the full moon until they shift.

I stand firm, my body poised and ready, and my opponents clench their fists around the hilt of their weapons with an air of arrogance. Three against one is a bad ratio when facing shapeshifters, and Keenan looks to have his hands full, as does the witch, so these three are all mine.

The saber becomes an extension of my being, and I am completely immersed in the battle as they rush in to slice me open, each of their swings finding nothing but air. Zooming forward, I hit the closest one with all my strength, and his sword tumbles to the ground with a metallic *clunk*.

His friend jumps and tries to stab me in the back, but I pirouette fast enough to avoid the tip of his blade. The one I disarmed roars as he tries to trample me like a ram, leading with his head. I jump as high as I can, high enough for the attack to only disturb the air below my soles, his futile attempt causing him to crash into the nearest car instead.

The saber's sharp edge finds flesh as I jut out my hand to wound the third one. Keenan immobilizes him in a rear-chokehold and snaps his neck, throwing me an encouraging nod. Fourteen down... three to go.

The witch slaps the demon that dented the car with her open palm, and an eerie vibration quakes the air. I stand frozen in disbelief, my eyes locked on the phenomenon before me—a strange and unsettling sight.

The man she just touched quivers as though he was struck by lightning, and he disintegrates, crumbling to dust right before my eyes. The particles hang in the air, suspended for a fleeting moment, before they disperse into nothingness—his clothes and gear dissolving with him.

A shiver runs down my spine, a mix of awe and unease washing over me. *That's not...normal.*

While I gape, the witch does the same to the second shapeshifter. I quickly sober up and use the distraction to stake an incoming vampire and behead him. His body vanishes into dust—though not in the horrific and efficient way I just witnessed—and his clothes fall on top of my feet.

Alana takes care of the third shifter, panting hard, her aura wavering in the dim light. Whatever forsaken magic she's been using, she doesn't have much left to spare.

I wrap my hand in the dead vampire's jacket and turn back to face Jasper's car. With a powerful punch, I smash the side window.

Alana stops me with one look and presses both palms to the door, the metal evaporating in thin air the same way her opponents did. The sudden vanishing of the door spooks Jasper, and he starts to move toward the back, but I take advantage of the gaping hole in the side of the vehicle to grasp his shirt and wrench him out.

With a hint of regret, I bury my aconite-coated dagger in his chest, up to the hilt, and slit his throat.

Instead of bursting into flakes of dust, my brother grins up at me with blood-tainted teeth. "Surprise."

My brows furrow, and for a moment, I think I missed his heart. *Wait... has he got some kind of protective enchantment?*

The prideful, victorious gleam in his eyes chills my bones.

"You're not Jasper." Doom settles in my chest.

The decoy is a perfect copy, down to the last hair on his head, but the demon digging my dagger out of his heart is not my brother. The witch once again uses her dusting power, the shape shifter's face stuck in a grimace before he poofs out of existence. That last kill leaves her with her hands on her knees, gasping for breath while Keenan finishes off a sniper that wasn't as dead as he'd intended.

I canvas the hangar, but my brother is nowhere in sight. I hone in on the sound of his familiar heartbeat, and my stomach lurches. It only takes one... While the faux-Jasper distracted me, the real Jasper managed to get on the plane, and the click of the latch being locked from the inside echoes deep in my bones.

# CHAPTER 8

# BLINK

## LEO

Jasper Beaumont seals the door behind him, a nasty grin spreading to his lips. "Hello."

The vampire doesn't even flinch as I shoot him square in the head. His flesh spits out the bullet as he prowls closer to me and Thom, the both of us guarding the princess—or at least trying to.

My new friend discards his gun in favor of a sword and raises it in the air. "Stay back!"

I shoot Jasper again, but bullets appear to be nothing more than a tickle.

"Oh, I'm going to enjoy draining you dry." He turns to the queen, his interest in me forgotten.

Arielle stumbles to her feet, her teeth bared. "You're here for me, not them."

"That's true." His garnet eyes flash with glee. "The Pereiras were quite appalled by your behavior. They're demanding reparations. I'll be all too happy to bring them your ashes." He doesn't waste any time and raises his long sword.

The silvery edge flashes in the night, and I jump in front of my princess. I can't fight him, disarm him, or hope to gun him down, but I can be fodder for the blade. A nice piece of meat for the sword to sink into—maybe even get stuck in.

A solid wall appears in front of me, blasting me backward into the aisle. Keenan beat me to the punch, teleporting in front of us, his strategy about as reckless as mine. The angel takes the sword meant for the princess square in the chest with a guttural *oof*.

Before I can move, a transparent orb flies from Thom's grip and explodes at Jasper's feet. A blast of sweet, acrid smoke—horse-radish?—takes out Keenan, Arielle, and Jasper, my vision fogged by the device for a few seconds as I shuffle to my feet.

The smoke clears, and the demons writhe on their hands and knees, coughing as though they're drowning. Unbothered by it all, Thom pulls out the long sword from Keenan's body in one sweep before beheading Jasper with it.

I gape at my companion. "What the fuck was that?"

The angel spits out blood and staggers to his feet, visibly hurt. "Aconite."

Arielle grips the armrest of the nearest seat, crawling back to her feet with her back hunched, and I rush over to help her.

"Thank you," she croaks, spitting out a mouthful of saliva.

As I help her into the closest seat, the loud banging on the door suddenly becomes impossible to ignore, and I leap forward, skirting the injured angel's legs to open the latch.

Alec about carved a hole in the door, his nostrils flaring. The vampire flies past me to check on the princess.

"Don't worry, Beaumont. We won," Keenan grunts from the floor.

I lean on the panel in the short corridor leading to the cockpit, my heart hammering in my ears.

The clear pitch of Keenan's voice spooks me as he says, "The plane *reeks*... that stench will stick. Do ye know how hard it is to find cheap private jets?"

Thomas peeks at the witch through the porthole, and his spine eases. He offers Keenan a hand to get up. "You're welcome. For saving your life, I mean." He cracks a smile that's cocky enough to be considered mischievous. "And you can afford a new plane, I'm sure."

Keenan's face flashes with a hint of nostalgia... and maybe even affection? "Look at ye. Ye're not the angry boy I remember."

We all catch our breath. A handful of bodies pepper the concrete floor of the hangar, and I guess not all demons turn to dust when they die.

The redheaded witch elbows her way past Keenan and Thomas to the back of the plane where she stowed the rest of her stuff. "Good job, guys," she says.

Despite her victorious smile, her voice is not as energetic as it was earlier. Clearly, she doesn't trust us enough to show how tired she really is, but I'm not fooled.

Keenan's gaze bounces to her like a moth to a flame. "Ye leveled-up since I last saw you, Lana."

She shrugs his comment off, but not in an arrogant way, her lips pressed together in a thin line. "Not really. I just had the right set of tools. Funny how you still fight with only guns, blades, and teeth."

Alec glowers from his seat beside Arielle, his shadowy gaze full of reproach. "No self-respecting vampire would fight his own kind with the inventions of rebels."

Arielle sighs at his reaction and offers a slightly more diplomatic answer. "Alec means to say that, in the wrong hands, these types of weapons could cause a lot of damage. They allow normals to hunt us, and so they're outlawed by my kin."

Thomas chuckles darkly. "So... think we should just wait around until we're eaten?"

Alec clicks his tongue. "Eaten, really? From where I'm sitting, demons are the ones in danger. In the last century, human populations have skyrocketed. They outnumber demons 10000 to 1. We've got to keep our weaknesses a secret, or we'll be the ones going extinct, not them."

Arielle nods. "That's the true purpose of the night courts. Our rules are strict, but they make the world safer for all supernaturals." Her blue gaze darts to Alana. "Even witches."

The redhead purses her lips to the side like she's contemplating the vampire's point of view. "Hm, maybe. But until demons stop hunting us like we're venison, I'll keep my grenades close anyway." She zips up her bag and throws it over her shoulder. "Can I get a minute alone, Your Majesty?"

Arielle and Alana walk off the plane with Alec, the bodyguard inspecting the hangar once more as the queen discusses something with our new, reluctant ally.

Keenan walks over to me, erasing the others from my peripheral vision. The slash on his torso has already healed, the big splash of blood reddening his white t-shirt the only clue that he was stabbed straight through the chest as he grazes my cheek with his thumb. "Ye alright, leanbh?"

"Yes." Surprised by the gesture, I jolt away and run a hand through my hair, my gaze darting around the plane to check if someone saw us.

I cross Thomas' gaze and quickly look away, blood searing my cheeks.

I wasn't raised in a world where bisexuality was accepted and tried to live as though it wasn't a part of me. Besides... reciprocating Keenan's kiss was only a product of his enticing magic, nothing else. Both my fascination for Arielle and the angel derive from their demon-ness, and that fact alone is enough to whip me back to reality.

*I'm only a nice meal to them. Normals outnumber demons like livestock outnumber the farmers.*

*That's all.*

And if a part of them feels something more, it doesn't erase the fact that they feed from me, and that my first purpose is to please their taste buds. Needing a moment to myself, I hustle out of the plane.

Thomas is quick on my heels. "We're leaving soon... You should come with us."

I hold a hand out in his general direction, not meeting his inquisitive gaze. "I'm not a victim here. Don't get me wrong, I'm miserable, but there are a ton of variables... My family has been mixed up in this for centuries, you can't possibly understand—"

"Listen, I don't know what Keenan offered you, but you have other options, Leo. It's hard to be a normal, a simple human in this world when so many others have more power, but we could help you protect yourself *and* your family. You don't have to become like him."

My brows pull together, and my voice is low and dark as I say, "What?"

"I saw it in your eyes. When Keenan blinked in to save her, you envied him. It's perfectly natural, I envy him, too—"

"I don't know what you think you saw, but it's my business."

He raises both palms in front of him. "Hey, I just want to help."

"Help someone else, then," I bark, his unrelenting scrutiny starting to get under my skin. The man feels eerily familiar and pushes my buttons the way few strangers do, like we share some type of common ground I can't quite wrap my head around.

He scratches the back of his neck for a minute, his lips pursed in an apologetic pout. "Alright. Keenan has my number... if you change your mind. Take care, Leo."

His witch friend falls in step with him as he leaves, the two of them exchanging a few words of encouragement, and I watch them walk away with a giant boulder in my stomach. With everything going on, maybe Arielle would have agreed for me to join them. Maybe if I'd promised never to go back to Hadria and basically play dead, she would have set me free.

Maybe.

The guy slayed a vampire right in front of me like it was nothing, but I realize right then and there, I don't want to leave my vampire princess behind. Whatever I thought before, I don't want out of this fight now.

An intrusive, bitter doubt weasels its way into my brain as Thomas' sleek black Vanquish spits out gravel on its way out of the hangar. Am I making the biggest mistake of my life?

My gaze falls to the princess—the queen, now—and my chest warms. I made a promise to her. My mind flashes back to the night-fall ceremony, when she looked so small and vulnerable in her black, feathery dress. She's come a long way since then, but as long as she needs me, I will stay by her side.

Always.

# CHAPTER 9
# RISEN
## ARIELLE

The rain drums hard on the white tarp of the hangar, the thick cover of clouds shielding us from the morning sun as the witch's car disappears in the distance. Most of the dead bodies have already been dusted, but Alec inspects the clusters of clothes and personal effects left behind. I take his lead and search the glove compartment of the vehicle closest to me.

Leo grabs the opened passenger door. "What happens now?"

My first-blood looks exhausted, the blood loss he suffered in order to heal me dragging down his features. A red splatter mars the collar of his white shirt, the scar left over by Keenan's bite still red and swollen. I squint at the hideous mark, but the leather wallet I pull from the middle of the console provides a welcomed distraction.

"I found something." A calling card identifies the band of shapeshifters as being part of a gang. The hairy spider on its front brings chills to my neck, and I climb out of the SUV to show it to the others.

Keenan shakes his head in annoyance. "Damn Widow Makers."

I flip the card between my fingers. "I've heard of them. They're a ruthless band of mercenaries."

Alec pries the piece of paper from my hand and glares at it like he can somehow kill them a second time just by looking at their personal effects. "They've been particularly active in the USA lately, but yeah, mercenaries. Not the kind of company Jasper usually keeps."

A heavy weight presses on my shoulders. "Jasper probably hired the assassins that tried to kill me back in France, too. If he was involved from the beginning...maybe the entire government is corrupt."

Alec slides the ugly card inside his jacket. "Jasper didn't bring any of the crown's soldiers or guards, so he was still trying to keep this mission a secret. He let it slip that Peter thought you were dead. He orchestrated everything so you'd be married off to Pereira and permanently out of his way. Killing you was plan B. And I had no clue..." he trails off.

I stand on the tip of my toes and kiss his cheek, feeling like I want to curl into him and sleep half a year. "I know you didn't."

"No...you misunderstand. I'm saying I should have known. It was my job to know and protect you—"

"Hush. I won't let you beat yourself up over it." With a small sigh, I rest my forehead on his shoulder, unable to piece together all the threads of his brother's betrayal at the moment, my brain still fogged by the aftermath of the ritual.

"That's not all. Clearly, my brothers arranged to have the king killed, too," Alec adds bitterly.

My chest heaves at the news. "Jasper told you that?"

"He didn't have to." Alec rubs the arch of his brows with a shaky hand. "Jasper told me that Victor had been killed by a Zhao assassin, but if it was in fact a scheme, I bet Garrett was in on it, too."

Leo clears his throat. "We shouldn't make too many assumptions now, it's still too fresh."

I give him a small nod, grateful for his input. "Leo's right. We should go someplace safe, first, and think."

Alec's brother just died, and that must suck, whatever the circumstances.

I'm lucky to be alive. The evil necklace Pereira gave me attempted to steal my voice, my freedom, and my very breath. Now that I've got it back, I'm not going to let it go to waste.

But first, we need to rest...and feed.

Keenan yanks off a big tarp from a white, nondescript jeep. "Let's get on the road. I wasn't kidding when I said private jets were hard to come by, but I know where we can find a suitable one," he says with a hint of mischief as he climbs in behind the wheel.

Leo joins him in the front, leaving Alec and me in the back. He looks too pale, his usually strong, leathery scent watered down, and a hint of sweat glistens on his forehead. I lean forward to take a better look at him. "Are you alright, Leo?"

My first-blood hikes himself up on the seat, his fists clenched. "Not really, but I'm tired of being the guy that passes out all the time."

I squeeze his shoulder, guilt grating my insides. Without the magic supplements to help his red blood cells regenerate, Leo's in real danger. "I'm sorry I took too much blood. I owe you my life, Leo. You saved me."

"The witch saved you..." he glances sideways at Keenan. "Besides, you weren't the only one."

The angel's lips curl down in a pout. "We have to find ye someone else to feed from, Yer Highness. Chances are ye'll need more blood before sunset."

"I have to feed too, and soon." Alec declares, his grim expression spelling out exactly how fucked we would be if we had to fight another wave of shapeshifters or backstabbing vampires without sustenance.

Keenan chuckles under his breath as he drives out of the hangar and heads toward the regional road. "I'd forgotten how hungry ye bloodsuckers get."

Alec throws him a nasty look. "You drink blood, too."

"Only when I want to. I can still eat like a mortal," he boasts, and a hint of jealousy heats my chest. I would love to sink my teeth into a juicy piece of steak right about now, but alas...only blood will quench my thirst.

Keenan rummages through the glove compartment, his driving abilities not at all impaired as he inventories the contents before pressing a water bottle to Leo's chest. "Drink it all. It should help ye with the not-passing-out bit. And eat this." He hands one protein bar over to Leo and keeps the other one in his lap.

Leo gulps down the bottle and discards it at his feet. When he bites down on the chocolate-covered treat and chews, my stomach grumbles unhappily. "Alec is right. We need to find someone soon."

"We're in the middle of nowhere. How do you expect—" he stops abruptly, eyes focused on a car parked on the side of the road.

Two men looking to be in their early twenties are changing a flat tire, and Keenan smirks as he pulls up behind them. "Well, you guys are the luckiest bloodsuckers alive."

The metallic wrapping from the protein bar crinkles in Leo's hand. "Don't kill them. Please."

Alec leans into my ear. "I'll knock them out first, so they won't remember what happened. Don't step out, you're too weak to endure the sunlight, even if it's raining. I'll bring one of them to you."

My fangs pierce my gums. "Hurry."

The two men turn to look at Alec as he steps out of the car. The one closest to the bumper crosses his tattooed arms over his chest, but before he opens his mouth to speak, Alec's blurry form knocks him unconscious. The one cranking the jack stands up straight in alarm only to suffer the same fate.

The roof of my mouth itches as Alec totes him over to the place he just left vacant beside me like the six-foot-tall man weighs little more than a soda. I've never had to feed from someone other than Leo out of survival, but I need the power and the calories, and so I sink my teeth into the stranger's neck. Pressing my lids together, I concentrate on the blood and not my prey's sweaty armpits or his dirt-smeared hands, the taste of him sweet in the face of my bottomless thirst.

"What a nice place for a picnic," Keenan says flippantly, drumming his hands over the wheel.

Leo pushes his door open. "This is too weird." He steps out of the car and grips his blond hair.

Blood and violence...my vampire senses are dying for me to drain my prey dry, but I take only a mouthful or two more than I would have from Leo.

Once we're done, Alec returns the men to the safety of their car and climbs back in next to me. Keenan doesn't waste a moment before driving off, and Leo looks about ready to throw up.

Alec pats Leo's shoulder with a small grin. "Oh, don't be so glum, Callas. They'll be fine."

Leo flattens himself to the door in an attempt to put as much distance between him and Alec as possible. He looks as though he's just been bitten, the lines on his forehead making him look ten years older. "You know you'd never spoken to me before today, right? We're not *friends*."

Alec's eyes narrow, and his carefree, post-meal happy glow is promptly wiped from his features by a somber, almost predatory scowl. "You have a problem with me, human?"

"Your brother was a vile monster. I'm glad he's dead," Leo growls, his tone sharp and unforgiving.

I raise my palms in the air in a calming motion. "Both of you, please."

But Alec doesn't retaliate. Instead, he doubles-down on his meaningful glare, and speaks with such poise and strength that I shudder. "You know as well as I do that, before today, we were all still playing a part." He brings a hand to his chest. "I was the bodyguard. You were the servant. We might have both despised how we were stuck in these roles, but we played them. Now, we have to be there *for her*." He points in my direction, his eyes not leaving my first-blood. "I'm a vampire. I drink blood. That can't be helped. These men were young and strong. They'll wake up in a few hours. If you have a problem with that, you should have left with the witch and her human." Alec raises his brows like he's issuing the other man a dare. "Yes, I know they offered."

"What are you talking about?" I ask.

Leo's gaze flies to the ground.

"Thom offered to make Leo part of the deal. He thought we were holding him against his will," Alec explains.

Unease creeps into my full stomach, and the warm, delectable blood I ingested suddenly feels like a hard rock. "What?"

Leo still doesn't meet my gaze, the hunch of his shoulder speaking louder than words. The discussion we had yesterday, on the eve of my aborted wedding, is still fresh and raw. Leo's admission that he hated me for choosing him confirmed my worst fears. He hadn't volunteered to be my first-blood because he actually wanted the job. Now, I'm starting to understand exactly how he feels—like a discarded water bottle.

My heart breaks in my chest, my stomach in knots, the leftover taste of it suddenly sour and cold. I thought that Leo just needed time, I figured he wanted to take things slow as he adjusted to his new role... I never imagined his disdain for me—for my people—ran that deep.

# CHAPTER 10

# DOOMED

## ARIELLE

The Jeep's tinted windows protect us from the harsh midday sun, my vampire senses dulled by the rumbles of the car motor.

"I feel uneasy, letting him lead us," Alec whispers below the music, his comment pulling me from the brink of unconsciousness.

As if on cue, Keenan taps the console and tunes in to some classic rock radio station. He's driving us toward his next hideout—and hopefully our ride back to Europe. Considering what happened in the last few hours, I trust that the angel is on our side, but we still don't know what kind of reward he'll expect in return for his help.

His attention seems to be glued to the busy road, but I suspect his supernatural hearing might be as sensitive as ours.

After we stopped to feed, I took a short, unplanned nap, my cheek still numb from the kiss of the glass window. I rub it down to bring some life back into it and stifle a groan. Waking up with the sun at its zenith is about as unpleasant as a bee sting, and my body is begging me to go back to sleep.

"We can trust Keenan," I answer under my breath,

"I agree, but it still unnerves me."

"You just hate not being in charge," I tease him.

His lips quirk. "Touché."

The urge to nuzzle the space between his jaw and earlobe becomes impossible to ignore, and I lean into him, eager to continue my impromptu nap in his arms. His comforting scent threatens to lull me back to sleep as I rest my head on his shoulder.

The tight muscles in his arms tense at my unexpected display of affection, but my smooth bodyguard and stubborn lover quickly passes his hesitation off as an ill-timed stretching exercise.

I heard his thoughts earlier. He was angry with himself for setting off the necklace, but he better not get any ideas about keeping his distance *for my safety*. I won't allow that kind of crazy talk, and I meet his cautious gaze, trying to convey exactly that.

He glances down at his lap. "I'm going to get you home, my queen. I promise."

Without giving him the chance to argue, I slip my hand in his and twine our fingers together. "I know you will."

A victorious grin glazes my lips as he sighs in defeat and pulls me tight into his embrace, knowing he won't win this fight.

Leo's ribcage slowly rises and falls in the front passenger seat, and the sight of him so peaceful is bittersweet. I need to speak with him, and soon. Everything has changed overnight, and now that I am Queen, I will not let him suffer. Even though it means he'll leave me...

My throat shrinks at the thought, and tears well in my eyes.

Alec combs my hair away from my face, the gesture so gentle, I feel like I might break. "How do you feel about your brother's death? Truly?"

I swallow hard, a batch of red, sticky tears spilling over my lids. "I was so mad at him before we heard the news... I still feel I ought to fly over to France and yell at him, but he's gone. I guess it hasn't really sunk in yet." My family is gone. The Delacroix empire is crumbling, and I'm standing alone in the ruins of a dynasty that lasted two thousand years. It makes me feel both incensed and exhausted, and I hide my face in my palms. "Maybe it would be better to just...disappear."

Alec's hand glides down my arm in a soothing manner. "I've hunted my share of outcasts. You'd never be safe again."

A fresh batch of anger chases away my desperate train of thought. "I was joking—mostly. I will fight for my kingdom. To the death, if I have to." I crane my neck around to look him in the eyes. "What about you? We both lost a brother today."

A shadow passes over his handsome face. "Jasper was my brother by blood, but I barely knew him. Beaumonts aren't really big on family, except when it comes to intrigue and power. Jude is more of a brother to me than Garrett or Jasper ever were."

Anyone else might not be able to detect the trace of regret in his measured voice, but I do. Royals don't have a chosen family. We're meant to put blood first, always, but when blood goes sour, shouldn't we be able to choose who we keep by our side?

I squeeze his hand, thinking we were both slighted most by the people who should have had our backs. "Family's hard."

"Family's wretched." He checks his phone at that, the gesture meant to appear casual, but I detect a hint of moisture in his golden-rimmed eyes. "Jude and Bella are safe for now. They've taken refuge in the city."

A small smile escapes me. "I'm glad to hear it." I rest my head on his shoulder again, my heart in my throat. "Victor was manipulating me when he sent me to Brazil, but he was right about one thing. If we don't start to uphold our laws better, the shadow world will crumble. If we vampires keep fighting amongst ourselves, we'll just make it easier for another demonic faction to take control. I need to rally Peter Chastain to our cause. And maybe Garrett—"

"Jasper said that Peter thought you were dead, so that seems to indicate they weren't working together, but I don't know... He might have been lying."

It's the second time now that Alec's mentioned Jasper's odd comment about Peter, and it's...interesting. I don't see Peter as the type to hire an assassin. He already holds all the political cards, and my brother had already confirmed him as his Prime Minister. Why would he need to have him killed?

"We'll need more than words to test their true allegiances. I need to learn how to control my powers." I lower my voice even more, speaking directly into Alec's ear. "It's a rare opportunity, really. At first, I could only catch a random thought from you or Leo, but when I spoke to the witch using only my thoughts...something shifted."

He arches a curious brow.

"I think I could learn to control it better, instead of just picking up random thoughts. The same way you learned how to speak mentally with the other royal guards...it's there, close enough for me to taste it."

"Can you read my thoughts now?" Alec asks, his face wrinkling with a mix of worry and fear.

"I want to try something," I say quickly. His grimace spells out exactly how unappealing me probing around his private thoughts sounds, but I take hold of his hands. "Please. If I control it better, I won't invade your privacy by mistake and only use it on the people that deserve it. I swear."

This power could drive people away from me, even people I care about. Hell, I wouldn't want anyone hearing my private thoughts—that's just not a recipe for great relationships. But I'll have to test many loyalties and alliances to sit on the throne of shadows. "If I use it wisely, this power could make me a great queen."

"Oh...alright," Alec says begrudgingly.

We sit knee to knee, and he grips both my hands in his. "When we learned thought-speech, they stressed the importance of starting with eye contact."

His hands are both strong and soft in mine, and I'm struck by his willingness to help me despite his own preferences. "That could prove distracting. You have the most beautiful eyes."

His frown deepens for a moment like he's wondering if I'm being sarcastic, and he searches my face. Whatever he finds in my expression causes him to relax, and he cups my cheeks. "Thanks, Lucky."

The path between our two minds is strangely familiar, like finding an overgrown trail in the forest. Brambles obscure the path, but I just need to cut away the branches and thorns.

Alec pulls his brows together. *"1, 2, 3...testing. Humpty Dumpty sat on a wall..."* he thinks, the thoughts jumbling together like a waterfall of children's rhymes and sarcastic quips.

It's too easy.

"Is it working?" he asks on the verge of excitement.

"No. Think of something you'd never want me to know."

I concentrate on his irises, the golden rim incredibly beautiful and distracting. It takes me straight back to our night together, when he looked down at me with such care and awe. I shift, trying to concentrate on the task at hand and not on how I wish he'd climb back on top of me... As I extend my mind and push through, I keep bouncing off a wall of defense in Alec's mind, his thoughts veiled in shadows.

I squeeze his hands. "You're too nervous. It feels as though you're guarding your thoughts, knowing I could come in and steal them at any moment. Just...relax."

He gives me a quick nod and tugs on my hands, pulling me to him. "Give me a reason to relax."

A smile escapes him, and I grin in response, holding his hands tightly as he tries to slip them out of my grasp. "Nope. Ugh-ugh. You can't have these back for now."

"Why not?" He asks with a wolfish grin.

"Because you will use them to distract me."

His heavy gaze drops to the swell of my breasts, and he bends down to kiss the hollow of my neck. "I don't need my hands to distract you."

Keenan braces his arm around the passenger seat headrest. "Hey there. It's me, yer good old Celtic driver. Cut it out, or I swear I'll pull over and join ye."

Alec grins against my neck. "We better stop."

"I don't know. His threat's not the turn-off he wishes it to be." I wiggle my brows to make it clear that I'm joking. I'm curious about a lot of things, but having a threesome with Keenan while Leo is passed out in the front seat of the car is out of the question.

It takes a few minutes for Alec's breaths to settle down and the self-conscious frown to leave his face.

"I did hear your thoughts earlier... I heard that you didn't want to be King, and the phrase had such an unshakeable taste." My gaze flicks over to meet his. "Did you mean it?"

"Yes. I'm a lot of things, but I'm not cut out to reign. I'd be a horrendous king. And it's not just me being self-deprecating, I just... the politics of it all, the diplomacy skills needed... I'm a hunter first, Lucky. I enjoy working alone. You remember how explosive our first meeting was or how I treated Felipe Pereira. I have no finesse. War councils annoy me to no end and tribunals bore me to death. It's not a responsibility I think would fit me. I can tell it fits you, though," he adds with a hint of admiration. "You'll make a fantastic queen."

My heart aches at how certain he sounds, and the ramifications implied. Sure, we're nowhere near serious commitment territory, but I'm quickly falling in love with him. "It doesn't mean we can't be there for each other, you know."

"Doesn't it?"

"I don't plan on following the same old pattern of arranged marriages and empty relationships my family seems to have adopted. I want you by my side for what's to come, Alec."

He kisses me then. One kiss. A slow, disarming caress that leaves me more confused than before.

He starts playing absentmindedly with my hair, and his inner voice finally becomes clear enough for me to hear. *"Damn... I wish I could feel so hopeful. Peter is a kingmaker. He will fight for his legacy. The royal guards and a few ministers will rally behind us, but it won't be enough. If Garrett is the father of Adele's kids, he'll use his power over the army to seize control, and there will be war. Bloodshed. Even if we win, hundreds will die."* The bitterness lacing Alec's inner monologue shivers through me.

The mental images flanking his assertions are so vivid that I can taste blood on my tongue. Alec has seen his share of battles, and so many lives hang in the balance... I need to find a way for me to sit on my rightful throne without tearing my kingdom apart, or I'll be Queen of nothing.

Also, the unshakeable knowledge that he feels our relationship is doomed before it even starts hangs heavy in my chest. If he's so convinced that we've got no future together, how am I supposed to change his mind?

# CHAPTER 11
# ANCIENT HISTORY
## ARIELLE

S till reeling from Alec's silent admission, I reach between the front seats to dial down the music and offer Keenan a measured smile. The angel took a sword to the heart to save me, and his offer to join Alec and I in the back of the car earlier wasn't entirely in jest.

I'm no fool...he's not only attracted to Leo. "Tell me, K." His tongue darts out to lick his bottom lip at my new nickname for him, and I know I got his attention. "The murder-for-hire business must be flourishing on this continent given the state of the Pereira court."

I need to grasp the depths of our laws' demise on this side of the ocean, but Keenan being an outlaw himself, I doubt he'll be eager to admit to his crimes unless I give him a solid reason to.

"Do you have a particular question for me, my queen? Or are you just fishing?" The angel answers with a similar grin, his delightful aura luring me closer.

I find myself staring at his brown curls and wonder exactly how they'd feel between my fingers. "The Pereiras were certainly not eager to forfeit their comfort to uphold our laws, and if we're not careful, our entire species will be at risk."

Alec rubs the sharp angle of his jaw, his eyes narrowed slightly at our driver.

Keenan's gaze flicks over to me, his gaze as inviting and pure as a blue, endless summer sky. "There are plenty of other demons that would love nothing more than to claim the role of leader of the Shadow World."

"Mm...Starting with you and others of your kind, I bet?" I add with warmth, leaning ever closer. Alec's possessive grip on my waist keeps me from being swallowed by the angel's thrall and crawling onto his lap, but barely.

There's something to be said about the tug of everlasting peace... it's irresistible. Even demons crave a taste of heaven.

A genuine chuckle escapes the rugged celt. "Yes, I admit, my kind uphold the laws here. We offer retribution to the normals who have been wronged by our kind. Some of us step too far out of line and kill viciously. They're a threat to all of us...uncontrollable as mad dogs. They need to be put down," he explains with both confidence and regret. "We also offer security to those who need it most—hunted species or individuals that are hunted."

What Keenan is describing is a full-on parallel justice system. It would be unthinkable in Europe, but here... Just as Victor suspected, outlaws have flourished in the absence of a proper king.

I graze the shell of his ear, testing an attraction I'm still not sure is real—or if it's a direct consequence of his powers. "Is that what America has to offer? Hot cowboys and angel vigilantes?"

Keenan tightens his grip on the steering wheel. "Someone has to make sure that the existence of demons doesn't become public knowledge. Angels don't feed from just anyone. We offer peace to the dying and make sure the laws of Hatten are followed. The same laws you live by."

He's not wrong, but it's a slippery slope. If vampires become irrelevant, then so will our crowns.

I open my mouth to tell him so, but he adds, "But I admit, I was wrong about your family. I've lived through many empires, you see...

I've seen my share of rulers, both experienced and not, and witnessed first-hand how quickly the tides turned on some of them." His eyes cloud for a moment, allowing me to glimpse at the man behind the angelic facade, and the true force of his power trembles in my blood.

Keenan is old—older than any vampire I've ever met—and the depth of his deeply accented voice blows across my face like an arctic wind.

Alec carefully pulls me away from our driver, but the undercurrent of tension electrifying the air melts as quickly as it built.

"Don't be alarmed. I meant it as a compliment. Judging by what I've seen so far of their queen, your kingdom must be..." his ancient gaze roams me up and down, "...magnificent."

I swallow hard, trembling over Alec's lap, stunned by how much Keenan's words affected me. From anyone else, they would have rung fake or tacky, but not from him.

"Easy, bird." Alec growls, his stark tone heavy with resentment. "You're laying it on a little thick."

A certain melancholy washes over Keenan's serene features. "My kind is dying. I'll see you safe on yer throne, Yer Highness, and in exchange..." He looks longingly over to Leo, my first-blood still sleeping peacefully on the passenger seat. "Maybe ye'll help me convince this hauntingly beautiful man that being a demon isn't all that horrible."

Leo... A pang squeezes my chest at the thought that he might leave me. "Do you think he'll accept your offer?"

"There's very few drawbacks, really, for the ones that survive the change. Immortality, power, stamina—a taste for the occasional dying man." The angel grins from ear to ear. "I've only ever had one hold-out—Thomas—and I can't make his refusal a pattern. I'm willing to work for it. But you and I are not in competition. If Leo loves you—great. Immortality will sound even better to him."

I lick my lips, suddenly feeling faint. "And how many angels survive the change?"

"Don't look at me like that. More than 90% of us do, and Leo is a survivor, I can feel it."

"How many of you are there?" I ask.

He drags his index finger across his bottom lip. "I'm not answering that, but ballpark? Less than a hundred."

The news shakes Alec out of his aggressive stance, and the royal guard finally relaxes in his seat. "Less than a hundred...damn. You could teach us a thing or two about how to do more with less."

His words echo in my brain. *More with less... Maybe this fight doesn't need to become a blood bath.*

An almost insane idea weasels its way into my brain, and I turn to Alec. "Jasper told you that Peter thought I was dead? He didn't just imply it?" I ask, making sure I've got the details right.

"Yes."

I hold out my hand. "Give me your phone."

Sebastian called Alec to tell him about Victor's death, and he's still waiting for us to ring back. What better way to test Peter's true allegiance than to put his son in the middle of the battlefield?

The phone rings only once, and I can almost feel my childhood tormentor fuming on the other side of the line. "Fuck you, Beaumont! You could have returned—"

"Hello, Sebastian," I cut in, grinning at the length of his shocked silence.

"Princess." I don't think he's ever called me that, and the quietness in his voice quickens my breath. "You're alive."

My lids flutter at the obvious emotion lacing his words. *If the roles were reversed, and I thought Sebastian had died...By Nyx, I should have called him back as soon as I stepped foot on the plane.*

A cacophony of feedback booms over the line. "What in the— Fuck off!"

Thuds and static take over, and a few seconds later, Sebastian's string of curses becomes too faint for me to hear.

"Princess, this is Peter Chastain. I'm so glad to hear your voice.

Jasper Beaumont told me that you'd perished trying to escape your wedding."

"He's the one who perished, I'm afraid," I chime, counting the seconds down to Peter's response, trying to decipher if he's surprised to hear it—or at all annoyed by the ramifications.

"I can infer from your tone that he'd lost his way... Hurry home to us, princess, so we can discuss matters of succession."

"I am to be crowned queen, no?" I muse, taking note of his repetitive use of the word *princess*—which from the mouth of a talented politician is no coincidence.

I know how to read between the lines.

Peter is as congenial as ever when he answers, "Well, there aren't a lot of precedents here. Two kings being killed so quickly...the government needs to evaluate all the options."

I lick my lips, reigning my temper in. His measured voice doesn't fool me... he's already planning to overthrow my claim. "Alright. I'll see you soon, Peter."

"Wonderful."

The gears in my head turn, and the scandalous idea I've been secretly toying with imposes itself. I know what I have to do to be crowned queen, and—though it brings me no pleasure to admit—I can't do this alone.

I've been studying the ins and outs of politics long enough to know what I should do, and I set my trap as easily as a fisherman throws a net into the ocean. "But I'll pay my respect to our mother Nyx, first. In Hadria."

"Hadria isn't safe for you. You should hurry home, princess. The vote for the crown will be held in less than a week—"

"I'll see you in three days, Prime Minister." I hang up, letting him know that I won't let him rule over me. If Peter Chastain is as obsessed with his legacy as Alec thinks, he won't stand behind me over his own grandchildren—whoever their father is. If he gets an inkling of what I'm about to do, he'll try to stop it, but once it's done, he'll be powerless to change it.

Alec retrieves his phone from my outstretched hand and looks at me expectantly. "What did Peter say?"

"He plans to challenge me and put his oldest grandchild on the throne. Ludovic had no heirs, which made the succession simple. I'm a woman, so that muddies the water even more. I think Peter plans to take the regency for himself."

Alec shakes his head in anger and disbelief. "Tradition clearly dictates that vampires take precedence over bloodlings."

"Not always. I need as solid a claim as I can get. I need to make sure Peter votes for me."

The serious line of Alec's mouth stills my breath. "And how do you propose to get him on your side?"

I avert my gaze, suddenly feeling not as confident as I felt a minute ago. "I have a plan."

Nyx save me, I have an idea that might just bring the government —and Peter—to my side, despite his designs. I just have to keep it secret long enough for it to work.

## CHAPTER 12

# CRUEL

### ARIELLE

The Aegan sea rolls over the rocks, but its fury pales in comparison to the storm in my heart. The thick muscle at the center of my undead chest aches as I rush through the front door of Jason Delacroix's estate, a place I thought I'd left behind for good. Rain pounds on the paved stones of the balcony like it followed us here from the other continent, but the repetitive pitter-patter is not quite loud enough to drown out the sound of Leo's heartbeats, the pulse of his anguish palpable.

I instinctively reach for his hand and give it a good squeeze. "I'll meet you in my room in an hour. You should rest."

It's still dark, but I'll need to feed before dawn. There's too much to do, and I don't expect to sleep today. I can't afford to be hungry on top of it all.

A languid ache encircles my ribcage as Leo slips past our host and vanishes down the servant stairwell, not exactly looking forward to his reunion with the staff, I'm sure. It must be very difficult for him to be back on Hadria, where he effectively lost his freedom.

Being this close to home, to a living, breathing ghost of his old life, might complicate things even further, and the least I can do is give him a little time to rest before I expose my plans to him.

I gave the courtesy of calling ahead, so Jason is not totally thrown by our arrival, but he still looks lost as he clears his throat. "Welcome back to Hadria, princess."

"Queen," Alec corrects him. It's not completely accurate, yet, but people have a tendency to believe what we tell them to be true.

"Welcome, my queen," Jason corrects himself, knowing better than to antagonize a pissed-off royal guard.

I serve him a respectful nod. The dubious greeting confirms that I don't have his true allegiance yet, a fact I'm hoping to change during my visit.

It's weird to be back in Hadria, to an almost immutable piece of the night court, after so many hours in limbo. Out there, I didn't have to pretend to be anything more than what I am. I didn't have to worry about the gossip and possible consequences of an intimate affair with my bodyguard.

I didn't have to wear a queen's mask.

Jason is a rook on my chessboard, a piece inexperienced players could consider second-tier or superfluous because it's rarely used at the beginning of the game, but he's actually a vital cog toward victory.

He's been master of the island for decades, long enough for the humans not to remember his predecessor, and he's adapted with shrewd accuracy to the new age. Given the choice, he will remain in the background of politics, but with him on my side, my opponents are most likely to accept their defeat.

Jason's gaze bounces nervously to Keenan, the angel's wet shirt almost transparent and offering a most distracting view. Jason's first-blood offers us a fresh white towel to pat off the rain.

"Thank you, Jean. This is Keenan Maccaillin, my guest. Can you make sure he gets a chance to wash off and eat?"

The butler bows to the waist. "Of course, Your Grace."

Both men leave through the same passage as Leo did, and I turn

73

back to Jason, the vampire a little less on edge without the angel present. "Is Sebastian here, yet?"

By my calculations, Peter's rogue son should have already arrived.

"Are we expecting him, Your Grace?" Jasons asks with a frown.

"You certainly aren't, but she is." A boisterous voice thunders behind us, and I crane my neck around in time to see Sebastian stroll inside with no concern for his disheveled appearance—or his drenched midnight-blue suit. Water slicks his red hair back over his head, its usual fiery shade darkened by the rain.

I expect him to taunt me, but he just bends the knee, his head slightly tilted to the side. "My queen."

"Now he somehow hasn't forgotten his manners," Alec whispers for Jason's benefit.

A hiccup threatens to break my collected exterior at Sebastian's formal greeting, the solemn glint burning in his eyes telling me he's not being factitious. Even though his clothes are soaked through, he looks completely in control, and I know I've made the right decision, luring him here.

"But—will your father back her claim to the throne?" Jason stutters.

Ha! This is exactly what I'd hoped for. Jason assumes that Peter runs the show, and while that's mostly true, just having his son here plants a seed of doubt.

I motion for Sebastian to rise to his feet, my gaze glued to him and his damn perfect poise. "Leave us, I need to speak with Sebastian alone."

Jason's spine stiffens, but he offers me a quick bow and exits the room, probably running off to discuss the new developments with his wife, Emilia.

I keep myself from wringing my hands and turn to Alec with a soft gaze I hope conveys my repentance. "You too, Alec."

The bodyguard digs his toes in the ground, his eyes draped in shadows. "Are you serious?"

"Yes."

I couldn't let Alec in on my plan during the plane ride over here. Mostly because my bodyguard obstinately refused for us to be alone together, as though he feared that it would somehow latch the fidelity collar back around my neck. But if I'm being honest, his stubbornness was not the only reason for my silence.

Maybe I was afraid of his reaction. Maybe a part of me still can't believe I'm about to do something so... reckless.

Our gazes lock, and I swallow hard at the obvious betrayal shining in his eyes. His boots clomp along the paved stones, each dull *thud* making my heart squirm.

Sebastian watches Alec's retreating back with barely-contained glee, his feline smile stretching into evil territory. "Alone at last."

I put on my best queenly mask, one I wasn't even sure I possessed before I saw him. "You got my invitation."

The redheaded vampire, the same one who spent the better part of a year plotting new ways to torment me, prowls forward. "Invitation? I only overheard you saying to my father that you planned to stop by the island."

My pulse quickens under his stare. Only Sebastian Chastain can look so charismatic while standing in a puddle of rain. There's nothing simple about him, his love for rebellion and showmanship only rivaled by his thirst for revenge.

My lips quirk at his childishness. "Don't play dumb. As soon as you heard, you snuck out of the castle and flew here as quickly as you could."

"Did I?"

"Yes. I wanted you to." I say with enough confidence to rattle the most stoic of audiences. "I knew you remembered my mother's prophecy."

"One day, you'll want something from my daughter, and most importantly, she'll need the world from you," he chimes, imitating my mother's solemn tone. "When that day comes, you shall go to her on Hadria."

I flash him a genuine smile, knowing I could count on his sharp mind to piece two and two together. "Yes. How could you forget?"

Mother would scold us as children, whenever we'd get rowdy or mean with each other, and warn us that one day we'd need each other. She told us that when that day came, we should meet on the island. That was before her death, of course, before I knew she could foretell the future. I'd never told another living soul about that prophecy, but I knew that my mother had enough of an impact on the young bloodling for him to remember, too.

I look down my nose at him, head held high. Last time we saw each other, he taught me how to bite and prompted me to defy all conventions... he's not about to disappoint me now. "You know why I called. You know what I need."

His eyes dance with mischief and anticipation. "Am I really that calculated?"

"Yes."

All false pretenses drain from his face, and he looks at me up and down like he's measuring my resolve. "Alright. We'll get married, but I warn you; I'm not very domestic."

"That's fine." I tame the butterflies in my stomach to submission and offer him a nonchalant shrug. "I don't plan on being domestic either. We can just pretend—"

He slinks closer to me, quickly enough for my beastly instincts to kick into gear. I raise a hand to shove him away but end up with my palm pressed flush to his chest.

His fingers curl around my wrist, our noses an inch apart. "Oh, you can be sure of one thing, Lil' Bit. I'd never *pretend* with you." He wraps a hand around my throat, the ball of his thumb pressed to the hollow of my neck. "If you want to do this, we're going to go *all the way*." His last words sound dirtier than if he'd cussed.

I test my newfound power to see if he's in earnest, a part of me scared to fall for his antics again.

*"No fake-ass, sexless marriage. If she wants me in name only, she can*

*forget it,"* he thinks, surprising me. *"Together, we could bring the world to its knees."*

I thought he'd agree for our wedding to be just for show, but that's not at all what he's offering. What I find in his mind is nothing but a savage hope for me to accept, and my eyes flick to his full lips. "Done."

The wicked curve of his mouth dares me to make the first move, and I seal my proposal with a kiss.

Sebastian kisses me back like he wants to swallow me whole. Water drips along my thighs as he presses me hard against him, his wet jacket squeezed between us. I peel it from his shoulders, the shirt underneath not much better, the drenched fabric clinging to his skin. Feeling dauntless, I graze the ridges of his sculpted abs, coaxing an open-mouthed smile out of him, and soon enough, I'm about as wet as he is.

His eyes darken, fixed on the roundness of my breasts, the entire shape of them perfectly visible through the wet v-neck black dress. Cold water drips between them, my nipples hard and sensitive.

When he moves to close his hand over the heavy flesh in the same careless way he picks apples out of a tree, I skip backward. "Enough."

"Are you really such a tease?" he asks breathlessly.

The boyish pout on his rogue face melts my fears, the weight of the last few days lifting as though they were nothing more than an unpleasant dream. With Sebastian looking at me the way he does... I feel like the mask might not be a mask at all. This man held my heart way before I knew anything about politics—or sex. He might not love me the way I've always wanted him to, but he craves my body, and that's enough.

I mold myself to him. "What are you complaining about? You have the wedding night to look forward to."

"And when will that be?"

"Tonight at sunset."

He grips my waist like he's holding the edge of a cliff. "So eager."

I tug on his tie in a chastising manner. "I will tell Leo and Alec while you smooth things over with Jason and Emilia. No one else should know about this until a couple of hours before it happens."

His gaze darts to the closed doors at my back, and he lowers his voice. "Do you think they suspect what we're planning to do?"

"I think they would be fools not to, but it's not in their best interest to stop this wedding. The alternative puts them at a disadvantage. They're not big on politics, and me on the throne works better for them than a regent."

His eyes gleam in the night, red as blood. "I like this look on you."

"I'm not a little girl anymore."

He squints at me as though he's seeing me, truly seeing me, for the first time. "No, you're not." He curls a hand around my neck, pulling me to him, our lips a hair apart. "In the shadow world, creatures respond to blood and pain. The real question, my dark rose, is are you cruel enough to reign?"

# CHAPTER 13
# DIAMOND
## LEO

Hadria never changes. Every islander wishes for time to stop when they leave for the mainland, longing for the comfort and reassurance to find their childhood world unchanged when they visit, but in my case, it's actually true. Hadria is one of the few places both cursed and protected by demons, and the locals traded in the thrills of modern life for security.

Tourists seldom visit here, the whole island is owned by the Delacroix, big commerce and hotel chains barred from entering our world. Crime is nonexistent, aside from the occasional pleasure bite gone wrong, far-between incidents that spark gossip and curious whispers more than uproar.

As I was growing up, I would hear the stories... I even sneaked into a bar one night to catch a glimpse of a vampire, but I'd never imagined I'd be the subject of those tattle tales myself.

It's unreal to be back.

The princess' mark at the back of my ear heats up in the morning sun, and I rub it down absent-mindedly as I weave through the deserted streets to reach the town square. It's too early for children to run through the maze of back alleys behind the shops. The smell of fresh bread embalms the air, coming from Antoine's bakery, bringing back vivid memories of the countless times I ran to the little school tucked behind the church.

Old-timer Luke stops sweeping his front steps as I walk by. Deep wrinkles appear at the corner of his eyes, and he removes his hat, greeting me with respect, his other hand clenched around the handle of his broom. I pick up the pace and rush up the first flight of steps leading up the hill when a familiar head of blonde hair stops me dead in my tracks.

At the top of the white steps leading to the library perched above the square stands my ex-fiancé, her back to me as she struggles to twist her keys into the library's front door.

I didn't expect to see Zara again. After all, she lived in our apartment on the mainland, eager to finish her bachelor degree in history. She hates visiting the island, and for a moment, I wonder if I'm hallucinating.

She drops her keys, and the heavy bunch falls to the street with a loud *thunk*. Zara curses under her breath, and the familiarity of her voice slashes through me like a whip of thunder. A flashy diamond shines on her left hand and turns my legs to lead.

I hear nothing. See nothing. Feel nothing.

Numb to the core, I stare at the ring on her finger without blinking, frozen in place while she hurries down the three little steps and bends to pick up her keychain. The motion causes her to turn, and she freezes, her keys forgotten on the ground as she stands back up.

"Leo! What—How?" She tilts her head to the side, tip-toeing closer like she can't believe what she's seeing either.

Air blows out of my lungs, and my soles scratch on the stone pavement. I take a hurried step backward.

"Leo?"

I shake off the urge to run. "We're staying on the island for a few days."

She stares at me, her voice thick with disbelief. "I didn't expect—"

"Clearly," I clip, unable to look away from the diamond.

She brings her left hand to her chest as though she's been stung, covering up the fancy, overstated stone. Her eyes drop to the ground. "It's not—"

"I can't stay and chat. Mum's waiting for me." I summon a polite smile, my lips hurting from the effort, and climb the steps two at a time.

*Don't follow me. Don't follow me. Don't—*

"Leo, wait!"

My heart hammers in my chest, useless and exhausted. I want to scream. I've been gone less than a month, how can she have moved on already? How can she be *engaged*?

I pause and spin around, already several steps higher than her, the shadows of the building ending right in front of her feet. She tents her hand and holds it above her eyes to shield herself from the sun. "It—it just happened."

"You live your life, Zara. I'm happy for you."

It flows out of my mouth smoother than I could have hoped for, my clenched fists the only physical clue that I'm about to explode.

I told her to forget about me.

I told her to go and live her life.

I just didn't expect her to do it so soon, and I wanted her miles away from this island.

Leaving her stone-cold in the middle of town square, I continue my ascension to the very tip of the hill where Mum's house is located, the familiar path encumbered with painful memories, but not so hurtful as the sight of Zara and her big-ass engagement ring.

*She always said she preferred small diamonds...*

I was wrong before. Everything has changed.

Kit, the tabby neighborhood cat, snakes between my legs as I knock softly on my childhood home door to spare Mum a scare. At this hour, she's probably already done with breakfast. She hasn't managed to sleep past five since the cancer returned, and so it surprises me when it takes a minute for her to open the door.

"Leo!" A red robe is wrapped around her frame, and her eyes are sticky with sleep, but she quickly waves me inside. "Why are you knocking on the door like a stranger? You gave me a fright. Come in."

*Oh my god.* She's gained at least a stone, and the chalky tint of her skin is gone.

My next breath comes hurried and rash. "You look... amazing."

"I feel amazing." She smiles a smile I thought was gone forever. The smile of a forty-four year-old woman who's still got decades to live.

"Oh, Mum," my voice cracks, the joy of seeing her well and healthy melting away the shock and anger I carried here with me.

She wraps her arms around my frame without shaking, her grip ten times as strong as it was, and my heart swells to the size of a sun. Tears mist my eyes, and I crush her in a hug.

*I did this for a reason. It worked. My old life might be dead, but Mum is safe.*

Nothing else matters.

She rubs the tears off my wet cheeks with her thumbs. "Are you okay, λεβέντη μου? You look like you've seen a ghost."

I open my mouth to lie but think better of it. "I just saw Zara in the village."

Her lips thin. "That girl didn't wait a moon before she replaced you."

A defeated sigh wheezes out of my throat. "Who?"

"Don't bother with such details." Mum spins around and grips the coffee grinder.

*Details?* I arch a brow at her reaction. There is only one man on the island I hate enough for my mother to not be straight with me. Glenn Floyd, of course, and my jaw clenches at the news. The dude probably courted my ex-fiancé to get back at me for stealing his job.

Mum waves away the subject with a dismissive hand. "What

about you? How was France? Are you adjusting well? Is the princess as pretty as they say?"

I look at Mum again, imprinting all the incredible changes I'd once lost hope for. Her sandy-blond hair is growing back, her cheeks rosy, and I decide then and there not to wipe the smile off her face for any reason. "The princess is beautiful, kind, and brave."

And I don't even have to lie.

"Hello?" a melodic voice chimes from the doorway.

Mum and I both stare at the apparition. A white summer dress flows down Arielle's slender body, and a matching scarf covers her arms. Big sunglasses protect her vampire eyes from the sun, but she looks so...human.

She holds her wide brimmed hat with one hand and bends down to caress Kit. The cat rubs along her leg, his back arched, his loud purrs rumbling through the silence.

The initial shock recedes, and Mum adjusts the sash of her robe self-consciously. "Your Highness, it's an honor to receive you in my home. I didn't expect—"

I squint at Arielle, stunned that she followed me here, and more than a little annoyed. "Why are you here?"

"Leo Callas, mind your tone." Mum smiles at Arielle. "Do you want anything to drink? By Nyx...I'm a foolish woman, you drink blood, of course, I—"

Arielle chuckles warmly. "I'm sorry to barge in. I shouldn't impose on you, but I wanted to speak with Leo in private, away from prying ears."

I check the stoop, but Beaumont isn't sulking outside, and I usher Arielle away from the door and deeper into the kitchen. "Are you alone? You could be in danger." I peek at the empty street, suddenly feeling like my hometown is not so safe.

"I don't think anyone expects me to walk about the village in broad daylight."

"You shouldn't have come alone."

She removes her sunglasses and sets them on the table. "I'm not alone. I'm with you."

Mum's gaze bounces between us, and her eyes widen slightly, the flush of her cheeks deepening. "I'll leave you two to talk. I started working again, and I need to open the shop, unless... I can call Franscesca and tell her you're home."

"No need. I need to sleep. I live at night, now," I say.

"Of course." She grabs her shawl on the rack and slips her feet inside her sandals but pauses abruptly in the doorway. "Can I keep you for dinner, Leo?"

I sneak a glance over to Arielle. "I'm not sure—"

"Dinner. Absolutely. He'll be here."

"Thank you." She curtsies a few more times. "I'll see you soon, Leo."

My eyes narrow, and I clench my fists without really meaning to, a tinge of betrayal heating my chest. "You followed me."

She nods slowly, her eyes never leaving mine. "I had to discuss something with you."

"Couldn't it wait?"

"No."

The verve in her voice will not be denied, and I sit beside her at the kitchen table, our chairs facing one another.

Her blue eyes pulse with something foreign. Not doubt, exactly, nor shame, nor regret, but something equally dark and impossible to nail down. A flash of no return. "Leo, I'm getting married tonight."

## CHAPTER 14
# SET IT FREE
### ARIELLE

The words sink in, disbelief written in the bend of Leo's brows and the quizzical expression on his face. I skim his knuckles and watch his reaction, almost expecting him to flinch at the light touch, but he doesn't, giving me the courage to squeeze his hand.

"I want to be Queen, Leo. I want to change things for the better, and for that, I need to marry Sebastian Chastain."

"We just got you out of a wedding," he grumbles unhappily, scratching the back of his skull like the math doesn't quite add up.

I need to be more transparent, more open. "I want this. I'm doing it on my terms, for *me*. I want to uproot the very foundations of my court, but that can't be done in a day, and trying to do it alone is wishful thinking. I should be able to reign in my own right. I should be able to convince the government without schemes, but I will be Queen of nothing if I'm not realistic. Sebastian Chastain and I...have history. His family is most influential, and I need him by my side to claim my throne without *too* much violence."

Leo frowns at that last part, anger simmering at the surface of his words. "If you've already decided, why are you here?"

*Here goes. If you love something, set it free...*

"This whole experience has taught me something important. A monarch can't strong arm people into being loyal to them, and though I want you at my side for what's to come, I need you to have a choice. Some traditions will take decades to wind down, but I'm determined to be the one to put them to rest." I meet his gaze head-on. "Starting with you."

He opens his mouth to speak, but I beat him to the punch. I have to get it off my chest now, or I'll change my mind and cling to him until the end of time.

"I stole you away from your family, from the people who loved you. I never saw it as an issue because tradition taught me that it was the right way to live. That it was normal. They told me you were all volunteers, but you weren't. Not really. How many others ended up in your position? You're a slave, Leo, and I won't let you wither away in a life you never wanted."

"What are you saying?" he chokes, his face whiter than it was the night I almost drained him dry.

My voice cracks, my resolve fizzling out. "I'm saying you're no longer forced to serve me. I'm offering you freedom. No strings attached. You can have your life back or stay by my side... you can even go with Keenan...but that decision is yours and yours alone."

I said it. All of it. I feel both proud and heartbroken as I brace myself for impact, Leo's features slowly decomposing in an array of emotions I can't quite make sense of.

One thing is for sure: he's not smiling.

"Don't you need a first-blood?"

"I can hire someone else to take care of my staff—drink from a few different people instead of just one. Many vampires don't have a first-blood. Or lost them a long time ago."

"No," he declares.

I lick my lips, wondering what he's saying no to. I offered him an array of choices... No could mean a lot of things here, and I don't want to get my hopes up. "I might have to do a lot of hard things as queen, but I can't face eternity knowing that you hate me. I've got a chance to make things right—"

He storms to his feet, the chair careening to the ground behind him. "It's too late!"

I force my beast not to run after him, the need to sink my teeth inside him and make him mine again and deny everything I've just said quaking through my body.

With a low hiss, I glue my ass to the chair like my life depends on it. "You can start over. You can go back to your old job, or find a new one."

He braces his arms on both sides of the sink, leaning forward, and stares off through the opened window, his chest heaving as though he can't quite breathe anymore. "I can't."

I rise to my feet, the need to go to him trampling all reason. "Why not?"

He spins around, panting hard, and I hold back a few inches, my fangs tingling my gums.

"Because of you!" he rasps angrily.

Without another word, Leo crushes his lips to mine. The stormy kiss is hurried and desperate, and it knocks the wind out of me.

It's a loud argument. A declaration.

We lose ourselves in each other in the sunny kitchen of his mother's house, the sugary taste of lemonade still glazing his warm lips. A drugging sense of urgency spices up the air, and I stand on the tip of my toes, my feet slipping from my sandals. He hoists me up on the small kitchen table, the skirt of my loose summer dress riding up to my hips, and I make space for him, eager to be cocooned in his warmth.

He buries a hand in my dark mane, and his hot lips dip to kiss the swell of my breasts. I arch my back, my nipples hard and sensitive as he loosens the white ribbons of my front corset, one passionate tug at a time.

The dull thump of a knock is followed by the squeak of the front door swinging open. "Leo? Leo, please, I need to—"

I hop to my feet and straighten my dress over my exposed cleavage. Leo's arms fall at his side, his expression unreadable as he cranes his neck around to greet his unexpected guest.

The girl's gaze drops to the ground, her cheeks flushed and her heart wild as a hunted rabbit. Her curtsy is about the stiffest one I've ever seen. "Your Highness." Tears spill over her lids, and she struggles not to blink, her wide eyes almost glassy. "See? I was right about you. I'll see myself out."

Leo closes his eyes and rests his forehead on mine, his lips curled down.

"She was your girl?" I breathe, understanding the weight of what just happened. Only a blind vampire wouldn't have caught the huge ring on that girl's finger, and my heart breaks for him. And here I am, telling him I want to get married to someone else...

"Yes," he admits.

"And now she's not."

He tucks a loose, wavy strand of hair behind my ear. "Now she's not."

I spare a glance to the closed door his ex-fiancée just vanished through. "Do you want to run after her?"

"No."

A thrill shoots up my spine at the honesty in his tone, and guilt immediately quakes my chest. "I'm sorry."

He squints at me, his tall frame caging me in. "Are you really?"

I grip the table behind me. This is the man I met over brunch, the man who stole my breath and my heart with one sentence next to a fountain of champagne. With a sheepish smile, I caress my mark at the base of his ear. "No."

# CHAPTER 15

# MORE

## LEO

Arielle bites her bottom lip as I guide her to my old bedroom and close the door. I haven't lived here in years, and yet Mum never peeled the Green Day posters off the walls or threw out my off-scale sketches. My vampire queen doesn't look like she belongs here, the walls of the chalked house probably more brittle than her bones, her flawless porcelain skin vivid and bright compared to the washed-down fabric of my comforter.

Struggling to breathe, I lay her down on my bed and swallow her questions with a kiss.

I punished her. I got so good at it that I overlooked how badly I was punishing myself. I laid in bed at night fantasizing about a life that was never perfect to begin with, cursing vampires and brooding over the future I'd lost. I never once allowed myself to make the best of a bad situation and examine my true feelings.

My only goal was to be miserable, and I achieved that in spades.

Arielle came to my childhood home to offer me a complete do-over. My vampire princess, my queen. She's offering me the world... and I don't want it. I want *her*.

Her tongue eats away at my sanity with every passionate brush, her small hands tearing at my shirt and grazing the skin underneath.

I lied to myself. Blood rushes at my temples, my chest, my cock. I want to show her what blood does to a man. I'm dying to feel her curves and test how perfectly her full, round breasts fit in my hands. To see if her depths will feel as refreshing as her kiss.

The pin holding her hair up catches the sunrays filtering through my white curtains, and I pry it off her head. Her black waves cascade down her back, and I comb my fingers through the silky strands. I could have done it a dozen times, but I'd almost always chickened out. What a waste.

I begged her to keep the pleasure of the bite from me and refused the perks of this life. The truth was staring at me right in the face, but I was too proud to see it.

I could never be free of her.

She stole my life and my heart in one big swoop. Since that first intimate moment, when I held her against me and vowed to protect her forever, it was pointless to resist. Pointless to pretend she was just another vampire.

She owns me, but not because I'm her servant. She owns my soul because of who she is. Fierce and good and delicate. And I'm done being stubborn.

She's so fucking beautiful, her dark ringlets spilled across the duvet, her lips pink because of my heated kiss, her chest flushed with need and hunger.

"Spread your legs for me, princess." There's a bite in the word because I can't help myself. I'm still angry. I'm still broken. This might just stitch me back up.

She bites her lips and obeys.

I'm hard as fuck, my cock pressed tightly against her inner thigh.

The flowy silk skirt of her dress is so thin it's almost translucent, and I sneak my thumb under the lace guarding her sex. She's soaked through, her arousal pooling between her legs.

I wish I could go slow, but I'm bursting at the seams. The need to possess her as deep as she possesses me is stronger than anything.

My cock is warm and painful in my hand as I guide it toward her soaked entrance, the blood pulsing through it beat by beat. I push the lace aside and thrust into her in one fateful push.

"Leo. Oh, by Nyx, you're scorching hot!" She holds on to me with longing and desperation, and I move inside her, relishing her cries of pleasure.

I've read enough about my role in her life to know my blood will forever be her favorite, so I'm not too worried about her redheaded fiancé, or her deadly Alec... They can't ever compete with me.

They might have demon stamina or a hundred years of experience, but her beast craves *me*.

"Bite me. Like you did that time. Bite me like that."

She sinks her fangs into my neck, her drenched walls snug around my length. Everything throbs. My skin, my heart, my cock... All the way to the tip of my toes, the orgasm rocks me, one wave after another as I thrust inside her, over and over again, stretching her until her back arches and her screams become incoherent.

I'm right there at the crest of my own orgasm for *minutes*, the spell she cast over me leaving me ravenous. She flips me onto my back and drinks another mouthful of blood. The quakes in my belly subside, my dick greedy for more, still so hard it glistens in the morning light.

Arielle tosses me an evil grin. "Looks like you want more." She kisses her way down my chest.

When her mouth closes around me, wet and naughty and perfect, I grip a fist of her hair. "Fuck, yes."

She bobs up and down, her tongue darting out to tease the crown, and I hiss a series of curses and praises, almost out of my mind with the lust she incites in me, past caring about anything but the feel of her.

I relax on the mattress, making myself comfortable. A beautiful demon wants to suck me dry, and I'm going to enjoy every sinful, disastrous second.

# CHAPTER 16
# HANGING BY A MOMENT
## ARIELLE

Leo and I hold hands as we climb back up from the village to the top of the cliff where Jason's estate is located. We slept the afternoon away, nestled in each other's arms, and I feel like I can finally breathe again. My big hat and shawl protect my demon skin from the sun, its rays not as painful as they were just a week ago. My newborn skin, powers, and hormones are finally settling in.

Sebastian is tucked in the shadows of the entrance hall, chatting with a circle of servants. I'm surprised to find him awake, but the chatter dies down as soon as we draw near.

Leo releases my hand as my soon-to-be husband comes into view, and I reluctantly let him go, sure that Sebastian wouldn't have minded in the least, considering how eager he was to share his first-blood Fred with me.

The handsome vampire dismisses them with a quick whisper, and they filter out of the room by both exits, some of them heading outside while others take the servant stairwell down to the kitchens. With a satisfied look, Sebastian walks over to me and gathers both of my hands in his, the barely-veiled excitement gleaming in his garnet eyes setting loose a flurry of butterflies in my stomach. "There you are."

"Afraid I'd jilt you at the altar?" I crack, hoping to tame the budding elation in my chest to submission.

"You've already run away from one wedding this week. Just don't make it a habit." He raises my hands to his lips with an effortless, devilish charm that could melt the best armor-plated heart—even the heart of someone who's been burned by that very charm before. "I arranged for the ceremony to start exactly after the sun falls under the horizon."

"Arranged what, exactly?" I'd expected him to go along with whatever the Elder had in mind.

"It's a surprise."

A frown wrinkles my forehead despite my best effort. "I'm not that fond of surprises. Especially when you're involved."

"I promise you one thing, Lil' Bit. A life with me will never be boring." He sobers up a little, a shadow obscuring his face. "Jason and Emilia were a bit uneasy when I announced our plans, but they can't stop us now. There's no time for anyone from the palace to fly over here, and I think they genuinely would feel better to have you on the throne than a regent."

I squeeze his hand, delaying his departure. "And you're okay with not having a...traditional marriage?" I want to make sure he understands what I'm asking. "Pereira wanted a silent, faithful virgin. I'm not that." Without meaning to, I sneak a glance at Leo, my first-blood pretending to look at the paintings on the wall.

"That's good because I'm not a silent, faithful virgin either." Sebastian smiles a smile that reeks of sex and depravity, the kind of expression that tells me I've still got a lot to learn about the vampire version of him. My stomach flips-flops, but the fleeting expression melts into a genuine, almost boyish grin. "I'm looking forward to a life with the non-silent, non-faithful you."

His fingers ghost along my shoulder blade as he draws me in for a goodbye kiss, and I can almost taste the desire on his breath. Alec is all strength and muscles, Leo is warm, and shredded like a greek God, but Sebastian...

Sebastian is sin on legs.

"Hey, Leo," he greets the greek man as he breezes past him.

My first-blood clears his throat loudly. "Hi."

I swallow hard, unsure about anything but the languid ache between my legs. Fuck, it's like I'm in heat or something. The way Sebastian looked at me just now... the way he looked at Leo...

I can almost see the intense look he had on his face when he brought Fred to orgasm in front of me.

I tiptoe over to my first-blood. "Listen, I don't know how much of that you overheard..." If I was still human, my neck and cheeks would be flaming red by now, and I can't bring myself to look into his eyes, afraid he might be able to read all the kinky scenarios running through my mind.

"I don't know much right now. I'm not sure what to make of this blissful afternoon, or the fact that you're about to get married, but I know I want you, Arielle. As long as we haven't figured out what our lives could look like, I shouldn't make too many waves." He laces our fingers and gives my hand a good, heartwarming squeeze. "I'll go and make sure your Sebastian hasn't planned anything *too* crazy. And then I'll meet my mum for dinner."

I tug on his arm to keep him a while longer. "Promise me you'll think about my offer. It still stands, you know." *Even though it would crush me.*

"I will." He tucks a loose strand of hair behind my ear and kisses me goodbye before walking off to the servant stairwell.

The familiar hunch in his shoulders is gone, his steps confident and full of purpose. He doesn't look like the slave version of him I've come to know. Like he used to carry around the weight of the world on his back and is finally free of the load.

I veer toward the bedrooms to look for Alec.

Also, I have to find something that'll make a suitable wedding dress. In the past, I would have treated the dress as the single most important detail of the night, and designed one of my own, but time is of the essence. I'm almost to my old bedroom when a shadow obscures the corridor. Adrenaline spikes in my blood before I recognize Alec.

He spreads both arms on either side of him, blocking my path. "I just heard the news." The pained look on his face squeezes my belly. "Congratulations." The hollowness of his voice hurts me more than if he'd screamed.

"Shit...I meant to speak with you privately." I walk underneath his outstretched arm and open the door, gesturing for him to follow me, but he stays with his feet resolutely planted in the corridor. "Come in."

He snickers, shaking his head like I'm a traitor *and* a fool. "I just spoke with Jude on the phone, Your Highness. Him and Bella will be joining us in France."

Leaving the door ajar, I step forward. "Alec... talk to me."

"You left without an escort," Alec clips, his spine stiff. "You sneaked out without telling me."

"I was with Leo."

"I know. I found you soon enough, waited in the shade, and walked ten paces behind you as you came back," he enunciates like I'm an irresponsible child.

Did he really spend the entire afternoon under Leo's window, listening to us?

"You could have told me you were there," I say defensively, a bit cross that he didn't make his presence known. By Nyx... he spied on us having sex.

"It's my job to know where you are. *All* the time. Why would you sneak out like that? Why wouldn't you take me with you? I'm a grown man, Lucky, I know what the pleasure bite means to us, and I would never ask you to go without—" He chuckles under his breath, but the sound is everything but joyful. "I never expected us to be exclusive. Marrying Sebastian on the other hand..."

My jaw clenches, his obvious disappointment bordering on judgment. "Marrying Sebastian will rally the government."

"You don't have to marry anyone. You're queen in your own right, and my brother doesn't have a leg to stand on if we make it to court. Let them *see* you."

"I need you with me on this. Why give my enemies the chance to beat me if I can play a better hand and win it all in one sweep?"

"But you'll win on their terms, not yours."

"I know you're thinking about the consequences, too. We're on the brink of war, Alec. If I do this, it'll spare many lives, and what does it cost me, really?" He lets me approach him, and I gently guide him inside the bedroom, closing the door behind us. "Why can't I be both queen and marry someone I—"

Fire flashes in his eyes. "Someone you what?"

"Someone that'll make my claim to the throne undeniable," I say quickly.

"That's not what you were about to say." Dark circles are visible under his eyes, and he holds my gaze with a defeated sigh.

I slip closer. "I'm sick of death, Alec. If we seize power without weakening the kingdom, it'll be better for everyone." I stand on my tiptoes to kiss him, but he steps backward almost violently.

"You're not the first ruler who strives for peace. Who wants to play nice and avoid casualties and collateral damage. Nice doesn't last, Lucky. People are too nasty for that." His tone chills to the point of being icy. "And I'm not going to be your side-piece."

I raise a brow. "Kings have had mistresses for centuries, and they were treated well."

"It's different."

"Because you're a man?"

His tired eyes dart to the ground for a split second. "Well...Yeah."

"You told me point-blank that you did not want to become king. You just said you were fine with Leo..." I stare into his eyes, trying to discern if this is all about ego, or something else. "Are you saying that you don't want to be with me at all?"

"No! I—Leo is human. And I actually like the guy. Sebastian's not —" He rakes through his brown waves as though he expects to find the right word at the surface of his scalp. "Sebastian is too—"

"Sebastian," we both say at the same time.

I nudge his side, half playful, half scorn, and hold on to his jacket. "I should have told you first about the wedding. I screwed up. I'm sorry."

He looks down at me, long and hard, before saying, "Why didn't you?"

"I don't want this to end, Alec." I stretch up to graze his lips with my own, but he denies me.

A tearful chortle pops out of his mouth. "Then don't marry Sebastian Chastain."

"It's political chess. I need to make the smartest move here." I smooth down his turned-down collar, and goosebumps rise beneath my fingertips as I brush the tender flesh of his neck. "I'm marrying Sebastian in less than an hour, and we will find a way to make *this*" —I peck his lips—"work."

He shakes his head like the repetitive motion will somehow be enough to change my mind. "I won't let you do this." He grips my waist with enough passion to haul me away from this castle—this life.

In his arms, I feel like I don't need to be queen, but that's fucking dangerous.

"You won't let me? *Let* me? I didn't mean to read your thoughts back in the Jeep, but I did. You were about to deny me your affection *for my own good*. Is that what's going on? Do you think you were right about that, too?"

His jaw clenches at the outburst. "No."

"You let my brothers order you around *for years* like a wolf on a tight leash..." My chest heaves, the fury stirring up a buttload of emotion as I hook one finger around his tie and let it slide all the way down to his stomach. "You're arguing for my independence and yet fighting me on my own choices... you don't want to marry me, but I can't marry someone else... how does that make sense?"

"I apologize, *my queen*, but I don't agree with your decision." He looks dangerous as his hands follow the curves of my body to my ass. "Is there anything I can do to change your mind?"

I flash him a wicked grin, my beast loving the tint of desperation on him, craving the games we play together. "You have my permission to try, Mr. Beaumont."

*The dark gods know I've waited long enough for this...*

The sexual tension between us is about to melt my insides. Alec kneels in front of me and traces a fiery path up my bare thighs, the skirt of my summer dress allowing him plenty of access. The sex with Leo somehow left me needier than I was before, and I hold my breath as Alec rips my underwear from me and sinks two fingers inside my soaked entrance like he owns it.

"Who are you that wet for, Lucky?" he growls.

I have to admit this conversation planted quite a few ideas in my newborn vampire brain, but I can't admit to that. "You."

He removes his fingers, leaving me empty and calling my bluff.

"All three of you," I say softly.

He kisses my neck with a smirk. "Better. Don't lie to me. Not ever."

I love it when he gets all dark and dangerous. He looks ready to punish me for marrying another man, and I'm not at all against it. I've been dying to feel him inside me again since that aborted sexcapade on the roof. He stands tall in front of me, grabs the front of my dress, and tears it off me in one swift, dark motion.

I shudder in response, desperate for him to touch me. He curls up around my naked body like a snake. His hands drag across my naked stomach to my breasts, and my eyes snap open in surprise when he gives them a rough, unexpected pinch. I tear off his clothes in response, the impatience and anxiousness of my looming wedding somehow making everything more vivid. I trace the ridges of his stomach on my way down his sculpted body, and his abs clench when I grab his thick erection.

He grips my wrist, his golden-rimmed gaze beckoning. "No games. I need to take you *now*."

A yelp of surprise escapes me as he picks me up in his arms and kisses me until I forget to breathe. He spreads me out on the duvet and hikes my legs up to his right shoulder before he rams inside me without preamble, my legs held tightly together instead of spread, which makes the feel of his thrust even more potent.

Alec holds me at just the right angle to use my body for his pleasure, the desperate snaps of his hips driving me mad. *Fuck, so hot.*

It's a revenge fuck, but I'm about to implode, his length hitting that sweet spot inside me that makes me beg, stretching me over and over again. "Please, Alec."

The defined lines in his arms are mesmerizing as he picks up the pace. "I'm going to make you come so hard, you'll be thinking about me when you're with him."

His movements are a perfect mix of power and control. I can't get enough of him. What if he doesn't accept my choice?

This could be our last time together.

Somehow, the combination of his wild thrusts and being terrified of losing him pushes me over the edge, and Alec falls right along with me. We're left spent and shuddering in each other's arms, murmuring in prayer for a long minute, the violence of the sex rivaled only by the sweetness of the aftermath, his hands tangled in my hair, his lips soft on my throat.

My heart aches at the thought that this could be the end, and I push Alec over on the bed and climb on top of him, peppering his chest with kisses and settling in his arms like an explorer planting his flag in a newly claimed piece of land.

"Hum-hum," a loud throat-clearing sound resonates behind us. "We have to get you ready for the wedding, my queen," Emilia says from the doorway.

Two handmaidens spread on each side of her and sneak glances at the naked soldier below me, their cheeks heating up. Their blood pumps a little wilder, and they exchange knowing looks, a grin threatening to show on their faces. If I were a man, no one would bat an eyelash at this situation, so I decide to treat it as normal. This is not something to be ashamed of, and the double standard ends now.

"Give us another five minutes," I order softly, and they quickly disappear from view.

Alec's head falls back to the duvet. "You're really going through with this wedding?"

"Yes." I pepper kisses over his silvery scars, from his shoulder to his navel.

The sound of the tub slowly filling up in the adjoining room rumbles in my chest, and I know I have to leave the safety of his arms, but I can't quite bring myself to do it.

"Do you think you can get on board with my decision? I don't want to lose you, Alec." I press my nose to his. "Please."

"How could I say no to you?" There's a foreign softness in his words, but also a hint of resignation. "You're my queen," he adds with a grin, pulling me down for a slow, dreamy kiss.

I nuzzle the tender skin below his ear. "Play your cards right, Mr. Beaumont, and you might even get to walk me down the aisle."

He freezes under me. "Are you kidding?"

My stomach flips, and I bite my bottom lip, wondering if I was joking or not. I thought I was, but he looks up at me with this wild, vulnerable gaze... and I'm suddenly curious.

"What if I'm not? Would you do it?" I have no one to give me away, my immediate family is dead, and I haven't even had a second of peace to grieve that properly.

"Walk you down the aisle and give you away to that arrogant wise-ass?" he chucks out.

"Yes."

"You're asking for too much." He sits up, his hand soft on the nape of my neck as he whispers, "But I'll do it. For better or worse, I'm in love with you, Lucky."

The only cloud passing over this fucking perfect moment is the fact that Alec said it with a hint of regret. My jaw hangs open at his admission, and in this beautiful, fragile moment, I know that this man has to be mine. I will keep him by my side. Forever. "I love you, too."

We kiss again, and I'm tempted to slide him inside me again, but the curious glances of the servants tickle my naked back.

Alec rubs his face down, his demeanor melting into his professional, royal guard scowl. "I better go and get changed."

I kiss him one more time before he goes. "We'll make this work. I promise."

# CHAPTER 17
# NEARING THE EDGE
## ARIELLE

The strong wind blows my hair forward, and the dark strands fly around my heated face. I'm standing below the edge of the cliff where Sebastian arranged for the ceremony to take place, panting hard like I jogged to get here. The Elder, my betrothed, and our handful of guests are waiting for me at the top.

The edge of a cliff. At twilight. With nothing but dark waters waiting for us at the bottom.

How poetic.

I'm out of view for now, which gives me a minute to collect my thoughts. The fresh, salty air calms my nerves as I breathe in and out, more nervous than I was for my Nightfall—which is saying something.

Alec hides in the shade of the trellis, grapevines sagging above our head. He's wearing the same uniform he was wearing for my wedding to Pereira, the jacket freshly cleaned and pressed.

*He looks so fierce in that uniform...*

"You're...radiant, Lucky." His throat bobs, and the soft tremble of his voice softens my knees.

Emilia offered me a dozen lavish gowns, but I chose a short, light dress. The skirt finishes right above my knees and leaves my back bare, the long sleeves running down to my wrists.

My old handmaid, Selene, braided my hair to one side above my forehead and left the rest flowing down my shoulders, and Alec tucks a loose strand behind my ear. "You ready?"

"Yeah," I croak, hoping my nervous brain is amplifying the angst in his golden irises.

My lover offers me his arm, and I take it, my other hand clenched around a bouquet of black roses. The spiky ends of the stems scrape the lace of my white wedding dress.

The sun plunges under the horizon, and we start climbing the carved staircase leading up to the top. As we reach the last step, Sebastian comes into view. My soon-to-be husband stands in front of the Elder at the very edge of the cliff. His fire-red hair burns in the twilight, his hands at his front. A dark-blue tuxedo and white under-shirt highlight his strong shoulders, his expectant look turning my legs to jell-o.

Emilia holds out her hand for me to hand her the bouquet, while Jason, Keenan, and Hadria's Bringer, Jorge, stand on the other side of the rock. The four of them serve as our witnesses, but I wish Leo was here.

A steep chasm spreads all around us, the small nook barely large enough for the seven of us to stand on. Deep blue waves spray over the rocks below, their depths dizzying.

My heart aches, tight and painful. Sebastian still looks like sex on legs, but wrapped in an adoring prince charming bow, and the sight knocks the air out of my lungs. Alec guides me over to him, his game face on as he hands me over to the young rebel vampire and side steps to the left, still very close to us considering the narrow ledge we're standing on.

It's an unconventional wedding, but the fact that it takes place on Hadria—and with enough witnesses not to be considered *secret*—

will legitimize the proceedings. Any royal wedding would normally require the government's seal of approval, and I keep waiting for assassins or—Nyx forbid—the Prime Minister to jump in from the shadows and convince the Elder not to perform the ceremony.

"Isn't it a bit dramatic?" I murmur to Sebastian, trying to regain my composure.

The cliffs, the sea, the wind, the sunset...it's too much. Too perfect.

His lips twitch. "You wanted a traditional wedding in Hadria."

"I wanted to be near Nyx's tomb," I say, hanging tight to my rational side not to tear up.

"Nyx's tomb can wait." He takes my hands in his and eyes me up and down. "You're the loveliest bride in all the worlds, Ari."

My mouth is dry, but not with thirst. A moment ago, I was shaking with nerves, but now...now I can't remember why I ever thought I could marry anyone else.

My short heels twinkle, reflecting the sky's warm hues as I step closer to him.

The Elder draws in a long, measured breath, both arms raised to the sky. "We are gathered here today under Nyx's watchful eye to celebrate the union of our dark rose, Princess Arielle Delacroix, to Lord Sebastian Chastain, duke of Cimmeria."

*Oh my god. This is really happening.* I feel faint.

"Sebastian Pierre Chastain, do you take Arielle Beatrice Delacroix, princess of the night realm and heir to the shadow throne, to be your wife, in blood and death, to follow the command of our mother Nyx and protect her secrets until the salt of the earth covers your bones?"

"I do."

"And you, Arielle Beatrice Delacroix, do you take..." the Elder continues his speech, but I'm lost in Sebastian's gaze.

He leans in, his boyish grin turning my world inside-out. "It won't be all flowers and blood, you know."

"I count on you to keep my head in the game," I say quietly.

"I will, Lil' Bit. Until my last bite."

His nose brushes mine, the hand on the small of my back gentler than I expected as I look up at him through my eyelashes. He breathes me in, his eyes closed.

Sebastian's whole demeanor raises goosebumps on my neck and sparks a fire in my heart as his lips ghost over my cheek. "Your cue, Lil' Bit. He just asked if you wanted to marry me."

The Elder clears his throat, and I realize I was so focused on Sebastian I missed his speech completely.

"I do," I say quickly, my cheeks tingling.

The Elder relaxes, and I realize my long silence probably gave him—and everyone—the wrong idea. "You may kiss your bride."

There's no applause as we kiss, no sound at all but the rumble of the waves below.

The Elder joins his hands together in prayer. "May our mother bless your vows. I will take you to her chambers now."

Alec's ghastly glow is like a kick in the gut, his edges blurry. "I'm leaving. I can't—"

I hurry over to him at how agitated he looks and press a finger to his lips. "Stay."

"Jealousy is ugly, Beaumont." Sebastian cracks behind me.

"Shush." I turn back to Alec, his dark brown hair all disheveled, the energy rolling off him even wilder. "Stay."

"Why would I?" he clips, the dejection thick and raw.

"Because I'm your queen, and I need you."

My heels slip out of the satin pumps as I stretch to his height and kiss him hard under the pink sky. I don't have to choose between one or the other. I will have both of them by my side, and that's that.

Alec gasps in surprise. His hands flying to my waist to ward me off, his grip hard and unforgiving when he squeezes my sides instead, crushing me to him like I'm the only thing keeping him from jumping off the cliff.

Jason and Emilia have the tact to escort the Elder inside the castle, leaving us three to discuss our new *situation*.

Sebastian chuckles. "Well. That'll be interesting."

I'm a Delacroix. I can have my throne and my men. There's nothing to compromise.

# CHAPTER 18

# SEBASTIAN

## ARIELLE

Nyx's chamber is smaller than I remembered, my beast unhappy to be entombed in such a dark, narrow space, especially without a warm human to drink from. Whoever wrote that vampires sleep in coffins have never met a real vampire, I assure you.

I move deeper inside the stone room, my heart in my throat. What happened outside with Alec really tied a knot in my stomach. "Well... that was certainly an eventful ceremony."

"Ah! The Elder must still be scratching his head." Sebastian unfastens the knot in his tie and pulls on one end. The silk gives a soft *swish* as it glides along the crisp white collar of his shirt, his gaze glued to me.

I don't know what I expected would happen out there, but this marriage doesn't feel like a sham anymore. In fact, I'm not even sure I know the man in front of me.

The Sebastian I know would have made some flippant remarks during the ceremony, making sure to alienate the Elder as he gorged himself on booze—before and after. He'd say something crude about what we're about to do, so I don't know how to deal with the quiet, mischievous predator in front of me.

He catches me in his arms, his nose nudging mine, his gaze open and hypnotic. "Hey, Lil' Bit."

I barely keep my voice from trembling as I answer, "Hey."

He licks his lips like he's trying to find the right words, and the sight is....chilling. "I'm jealous of Beaumont," he finally chokes out, a shroud of darkness pulling his brows down.

"Jealousy is ugly, Sebastian," I quip.

"Mm, wise words." He cracks a smile at that and unbuttons his shirt. "But you care for him, yes?"

"I do."

"And how do I fit into this scenario?"

I twine our fingers and bring his ring to eye level. "Isn't it obvious? You're my husband."

He shakes his head like this is a big irony. "That must drive him mad."

"It does."

"So you'll... keep seeing him. Even though we're married."

It's my turn to frown. We talked openly about being non-exclusive... What is he getting at? "Like you said: you're not very domestic."

"I could be a little domestic. For you." He tosses his head to the side like it's a small, meaningless suggestion. "When you said we could pretend... I thought you meant something different."

I arch a brow, knowing better than to ask out loud. Sebastian is a tomcat. He'll rub his head on your offered hand, but you better not try to pet him before he's ready.

His dark eyes gleam in the night. "I thought you meant *I* could pretend."

"I'm not following."

He licks his lips in hesitation. "You used to *love me*, Lil' Bit."

My jaw hangs open, the instinct to deny it and protect my heart from him too strong to ignore. "I had a crush on you as a teenager—that hardly counts as something serious."

He pouts, but the light dancing in his eyes remains. "Still...You loved me."

"And you spent every waking hour designing new ways for me to stop," I add with a hint of bitterness.

"Did I succeed? Truly?"

*No.* "Pretty much."

"Then I'll just have to come up with new ways to make you love me again." He nods—mostly to himself—like this is an acceptable compromise.

You don't accidentally marry the man you pined over for years, and even if all logical signs point to the rationality of this alliance, I can't fool myself. Not when he looks so fine in a tuxedo, using a word I thought he considered blasphemy.

I keep focusing on his flaws, on the crueler aspects of his rebellion and all the ways he hurt me. It's a well-trained defense mechanism I developed after he left, a way to forget all the things he did *right*, like the countless times he sneaked into my bedroom to distract me with his crazy shenanigans after Mother's death, or how he covered for me with the Elders when I just needed to cry for an hour.

Oblivious to the weight of my epiphany, Sebastian holds me tighter. I'm left whiplashed by the entire conversation—and the feel of his arms around me. "You're on board? Just like that?"

"Sure. Why not? Healthy competition is good for the soul. Beaumont's always been my favorite royal guard—the only high-ranking officer with a sense of humor, so I understand, truly."

I bite my bottom lip, unsure if I can take him at his word. "Why did you accept my proposal? You hate all that has to do with the crown."

"You hope to burn down the court, no? The hypocrisy, the screwed-up power dynamics, the stupid traditions—-like the ones that say a woman can't rule without a man by her side? Or have three lovers at once?" He adds with a wise-ass grin.

"Yes."

He bends down to kiss me, our lips almost touching as he says, "Then by all means, my queen. Fetch me the matches."

EVEN THOUGH THEY'RE both vampires, Sebastian feels entirely different than Alec. The royal guard knows he's a great lover, and his movements are always rehearsed, his patience and skill allowing me to abandon myself completely to his touch without feeling self-conscious.

Sebastian fucks me with the verve of someone who has something to prove. He observes me with his brow bent in concentration like each of my releases is a contest he intends to win.

But what I love most about him is his dirty mind, his mouth whispering one scandalous line after another, driving me wild. He's known me my whole life. He remembers what fantasies kept me awake as a teenager and how deep my obsession for him went, and milks every inch of that knowledge to his advantage.

After five orgasms for me—two for him—he's still not ready to call for the chamber to be opened, and I call a truce, needing a moment to catch my breath.

So he decides to fuck with my mind instead.

"The year we spent Christmas in the alps... you looked so fine in that red dress," he says out of the blue, his kiss on my shoulder blade almost painful in contrast to his words.

I sit up, holding the sheet over my breasts. "Don't do that."

Lying on his side with his arm propped under his head, he raises an innocent brow. "Do what?"

"Don't try to rewrite the past. You thought I was ugly when we were growing up."

He squints at me like I'm the one that's being insincere. "Are you kidding?"

"I'm just saying. We can like each other now without you feeling obligated to alter your recollection of our childhood. I know you didn't think of me *like that*, and I've made my peace with it."

His head falls to the pillow, air blowing out of his mouth like I'm being unreasonable. "After I was exiled, I came to Hadria to see you."

I hold the sheet closer to my body. "You did not."

"I did. I saw you swimming with your little puppy dog, Lulu, and I realized I had to bide my time. Why do you think I came back to court just as you returned from the island?"

My blood races in my veins. "Ludovic had just died—it made sense for you to be there."

He shakes his head in denial. "I came to ask your brother for your hand, but he'd already set his plans in motion, and my father was only too happy to crush my hopes down, even though your marriage to Pereira didn't exactly please him either."

"Err—No."

"On Christmas Eve, when I hooked you with that ridiculous giant candy cane... I meant to kiss you, Ari. For real."

Cold sweat gathers on my neck. Christmas... my stomach squeezes at the memory. We shared our first kiss that night, right before he tore my heart out of my chest.

"You said that Henry had dared you to kiss the ugliest girl in the room," I grit through my teeth.

He shifts on the bed and clasps my hand, his eyes open and vulnerable. "I was an idiot. I couldn't handle saying goodbye to you, and I lashed out."

My pulse flies at that. "What are you saying?"

"I tried to push you out of my mind, Ari. I traveled the world, fucked all the humans, demons, vandellas, and witches I could find—"

I press my index finger to his mouth. "Shush. You're not helping your case."

"I did all that, but I couldn't get what you said out of my mind. You were right, Lil' Bit, when you told me I would always regret the way I treated you that night. I did—I do. I regret it *so* much," he adds softly.

Tears fill my eyes, but I refuse to blink, taking it all in. Sometimes, when something is too perfect, I just can't believe it's real. I'm tempted to look inside his mind to see if he's telling the truth, but that's a slippery slope. It feels real. Maybe that's all I need. Maybe I can truly trust him.

"I hate you a little bit for what you did. For letting me believe you could never be attracted to me," I admit, my voice full of unwanted cracks.

"I think you can see now that it was all bullshit from an arrogant, stubborn child. *Une petite peste.*"

My lips quirk up at Mother's nickname for him, which means "Little Pest."

"Why do you think your mother didn't just outright say we'd wed?" he asks.

I lie on my stomach, my elbows propped over his chest. "I don't know. Maybe she didn't exactly know what would happen. Maybe she was afraid telling us too much could alter the course of history." I play with my fingers, a smile curling my lips, and meet his gaze again. "Maybe she knew we were not in a place to hear it."

A small giggle escapes us both at how true that sounds, our childhood memories taking a life of their own.

"Did you know that Victor was gay?" I ask suddenly.

"Ah! Considering I found my father on his knees, blowing the daylights out of him, I'd say—yes."

My spine stiffens as I sit up. "When was this?"

He looks simply haunted, and my heart races in my chest at the angry curve of his mouth. "I was fourteen."

*Yikes!* I make a quick calculation in my head. Ludovic was way older than both of us, but Victor was closer to my age. When Sebastian was fourteen, my brother hadn't even had his nightfall, yet.

"That day, I realized it was all bullshit. They wanted us to study the sacred tomes and dress like obedient preppy dolls—" He slows down, tampering the torrent of emotions in his voice. "My father and the rest of the lords...they pretend to be these reasonable, important rulers that stand above the rest of the beasts, when in reality they are just better at hiding their sordid affairs."

*Oh, crap.* "Is that why your mother left?"

"I mean—would you have stayed with a man that preferred teenage boys to you? And then my father had the stupendous idea to marry his lover to his daughter, an arrangement I'm sure allowed them plenty of perks. If not for that, you and I would have been wed. It made way more sense, but he decided to please his dick instead. It's not like my sister was going to out her own husband and father, so she had to keep her mouth shut. Frankly, I'm surprised Adele hasn't jumped from the roof of the palace, yet."

I cover my mouth to hide how disgusted I feel that his father would do that. I'm just so shocked... "That wouldn't kill her, you know. It would just be really, really painful." *Oh my gods, stop talking. Stop talking now.*

Sebastian clicks his tongue at my half-assed attempt at dark humor. "It's a figure of speech."

"I'm sorry. My brain is just...imploding. But I think she's not as unhappy as we think. I think she's got someone, too."

His face creases with a butt-load of skepticism, our old snarky dynamic clearly not totally behind us. "Who?"

"Garrett Beaumont. For all we know, he could even be the father of her kids."

He whistles under his breath before staring off into the distance, his eyes draped in shadows. "*That,* I didn't know. It would make for an interesting argument in our favor..."

"Do you think we need it?" I'd rather not have to use the information, the thought of outing Adele's affair unpalatable at best.

My new husband seems to catch my unspoken question, and his eyes soften as he drapes an arm around me and pulls me closer. "Us? Looking so damn fine together? I don't think so."

# CHAPTER 19
# SIDE PIECE
## ALEC

"Congratulations to the bride and groom," Keenan says loudly, the angel's voice booming in cheer as he raises his glass for the happy couple.

The other guests around the dining table echo his sentiment, and I fight off the urge to roll my eyes and avert my gaze as Emilia goads them into a public kiss.

Dining with newlyweds when you're hot for the bride is awkward, to say the least. It's been twenty-four hours since the wedding. I tossed and turned in my bed all day after an entire night of misery, knowing Arielle was with the redhead, the sly vampire probably trying to fuck me out of her mind.

I grab my forehead at my train of thought. *You're losing it, man. Why didn't you want to be king, again? This could be you beside her, you moron.*

From the happy fucking grin on Sebastian's face, he certainly believes he succeeded. Him and his fucking wife are sitting on the other side of the table, but I can practically see his wicked hand sliding up her creamy thigh as we speak.

I bet he thinks he's better in bed than me, which is a big fucking farce.

I would normally be standing *behind them* and not be eating *with them*, but Arielle insisted for Keenan, Leo, and I to join them at the table for dinner. They skipped the reception last night and went straight for the *consummation* part, as is tradition for vampires. Jason and Emilia look confused by our presence, and the steak and eggs with a side of AB negative set me on edge. I'm a "drink from the vein and be on my way" kind of vampire, so the blood tasting throws me for a loop, the selection of forks next to my silver plate completely ridiculous.

*As if I'd ever prefer to eat with a three-pronged toy than a proper fork.*

"So...How did my dad take the news?" Sebastian asks Jason with a rogue smile that makes me want to punch his smug face.

Silence takes over the room for a moment, Jason's grip tight around his cup of blood. "I don't—What do you mean?"

Arielle and I exchange a glance. *"What is he getting at?"* I ask her telepathically, my unease growing when she answers with a discreet shrug.

Sebastian chuckles and sips on his cup, licking his bloody lips with a mix of humor and annoyance that only a high-born vampire can master so perfectly. "Oh come on, Jason. You called him as soon as the wedding was over. Covering your ass in case the vote goes against us."

The master of the island fails to mask a cringe.

Sebastian stuffs a big piece of rare steak in his mouth. "It's okay, dude. We can't expect you to defy the whole court for our sake. Still..." wickedness blazes in his garnet eyes. "How did he react?"

Jason pats his mouth down with his fancy cloth napkin, holding Sebastian in suspense for a moment. "He was...surprised."

"I thought your father would be thrilled. It's not every day your only son weds the heir to the throne," I say, my brows pulled together.

Sebastian's breezy smile is wiped from his face. "Don't talk about things you don't understand, Beaumont."

"Isn't that what he wanted for you all along?"

Arielle's eyes widen, and she warns me off the subject through thought-speech. *"Alec—"*

"No, I want to know why he's making that face." I gesture in Sebastian's direction, at a complete loss as to why marrying the princess would slight his father.

Determination flashes in her deep blue eyes. "Alec, let it go. It's none of your business."

My fists curl at my sides, my tongue pressed hard against the roof of my mouth. "Your wish is my command, Your Highness."

"Don't be like that."

"Isn't that my line?" I jump to my feet, throwing the cloth napkin over my untouched plate. "Requesting permission to take my leave, *my queen.*"

"Denied." She stands and dumps her golden cup on the nearest table. "Come with me." Her shoulders tucked in like she's fucking ashamed of my behavior, she leads me away from the dining room.

A searing heat encircles my ribs, my blood running cold as I shadow her to her bedroom.

She spins around, her anger tangible. "What the fuck was that?"

"You scolded me like a child."

"I was reading Jason's thoughts to make sure he's on our side. Sebastian was goading him into speaking about Peter in case—"

"Oh, I'm sorry I ruined your little snooping expedition. Maybe if you'd told me about it beforehand—"

She grabs her forehead like I'm the biggest ass on the planet. "Maybe if you'd been here this morning, I would have had the chance to tell you, but you were out, and I needed a good night's sleep after staying awake all day yesterday."

"You were in Nyx's tomb," *being plowed by another man.* "I had to take a breather."

"I'm not chastising you for taking a walk. I'm saying that's why I couldn't fill you in on our plan."

*Our* plan... *If she thinks I'll put up with this bullshit, she's dreaming.*

She doesn't own me, but her dark eyes are so fucking beautiful... I'm suffocating. I start ripping off my uniform, throwing the jacket at her head, then the tie.

"What are you doing?" The glacial fear in her voice should make me feel better, but it's not enough.

"I quit." I toss my ear piece and my gun over her bed, my chest heaving, quaking, *breaking* with every painful breath.

She wets her lips, meeting my stare head-on. "That's unacceptable."

I throw my hands in the air, my entire body shaking. "Then have me arrested, I don't care."

She slithers closer with grace and elegance, her previously annoyed frown morphing into a soft, loving gaze. "Nothing has to change."

"I'm not going to obey Sebastian fucking Chastain like a good little soldier, watch him touch you, kiss you in front of everyone while I have to sneak into your bed while he looks the other way, begging for scraps like a fucking chomp. I won't do it."

A heavy breath quakes her chest, and she stares into my eyes, her irises so blue I feel like I'm being swallowed by the sky. "I love you."

I choke on a bitter snort. "You're married to *him*."

"That doesn't change how I feel."

"What if I didn't look the other way?" Sebastian stalks in from the shadows, and my first instinct is to wrap myself around my queen, protecting her from danger. His eyes fall to my arms, wrapped tightly around her waist, and a wicked smile curves his lips. "She's *our* queen. If she wants both of us, who am I to deny her what she needs?"

I blink a few times, my coiled muscles relaxing one by one. He's not here to hurt her—or me, and the weight of his question rams into me like a truck. "Are you serious?"

His lewd smile melts into something more congenial—and definitely more honest. "Come on, Beaumont. I grew up at court. I know you're not against a few..." he moves his fanned hands from side to side, "blurred lines when it comes to sex."

I swallow hard at the truth in his words. I'm not sure why I'm suddenly acting like a jealous creep, ready to take my woman by the hair and drag her into my cave... it's not who I am.

Sebastian continues, oblivious to my change of heart. "We're all consenting adults. We would just be doing openly what countless others have been doing in the dark. Hell, we might be the first ones who even try to live as they truly are."

I lick my lips and choose my next words carefully. "You talk a good game, my lord."

He winces sheepishly at the formality. "I like you, Alec. I know I've been holding my title over you for as long as I've been alive, but I'm willing to stop. You're ten times the fighter I am. I needed something to boost my ego."

I gape at the admission, at a loss for words. Sebastian Chastain being a relationship anarchist shouldn't surprise me in the least, but somehow, I always figured the kid was all roar and no action. And I definitely never heard him utter a sincere apology before.

"We can change the way things are done for good. I'm talking about marrying women off to selfish pricks and denying them happiness. I'm talking about the countless servants your fiend of a younger brother *raped* just because he could, because he knew the truth about Victor and my father and used it to buy himself immunity. We don't have to be like them. Why should we be encouraged to fuck every warm human in the room but be prohibited from doing the same with a vampire we love? How does that make sense?"

Arielle stares at him with longing, surprise, and a tinge of excitement. She didn't put him up to this. Not in the least.

I'm not sure he knows exactly what he's signing up for, but I keep an open mind. "So you're proposing to tell everyone that she's cheating on you?"

"That we're together. The three of us."

He does a swirly motion with his finger, and I press my lips together not to laugh.

Making sure to look as unfazed and unimpressed as possible, I ask, "How would that work?"

"Are you asking what side of the bed I'd want? Or if I snore? I prefer the middle, and I don't snore, but I do talk in my sleep." He pauses for a long time, letting me absorb the ridiculousness of my question before adding, "Our queen needs me for my name and you for your raw, brute strength...your nice ass is only a bonus."

Somehow, him talking a load of crap does relax me. It shouldn't surprise me, either. I've always taken great pleasure in following his antics, and a genuine laugh escapes me. "Alright, alright. I'm showing my age, aren't I?"

"You're being a tiny bit of a bore, yes. We have to start some-where, and the three of us together is actually perfect. A Delacroix queen with both a Beaumont *and* a Chastain devoted to her? It might be the perfect political play. The people that could have been tempted to follow your brother's lead will get confused, and my dad will not advocate for his grandkids if they're illegitimate. Not when he could have *me* on the throne. I'm his blood. That's all he cares about." Sebastian extends his hand. "Are you in or out, Beaumont?"

I shake it with confidence. If the kid is ready to take on the entire court and their useless traditions, I'm not going to stand in his way. If we're both ready to work it out for her, I might even get excited about this...relationship? Throuple Threesome? Reverse harem?

His gaze flicks over to our queen, his expression switching from fierce to predatory. "She's wet as fuck. Can you smell her?"

The corner of my mouth curls up, and I follow his feral gaze. "Yes."

Arielle's chest heaves harder with each breath, her nipples perfectly visible through the front of her dress.

"Just the thought of us both touching her..."

Blood pumps in my veins, the beast inside me awakened by

Sebastian's filthy voice as he stalks closer to Arielle. Vampires hunt best in pairs. Earlier, I felt compelled to protect the queen, but her arousal acts as a powerful pheromone. Just like that, I'm a hunter again.

"What are you doing? We don't have time—"

Sebastian unfastens his belt and passes it to me. "Tie her up. Hands behind her back."

That's an order I'm happy to comply with. Hell, I'm getting way on board with his view of our newly-defined relationship. If he fucks half as fiercely as he lives... I blur over to Arielle and run my hands down her arms, bringing her wrists to her back and tying them together with the leather belt. The free end of the leather falls at her feet, the old-fashioned belt longer than the modern ones.

"You get both of us—and Leo as a bonus. You have to give us something in return," Sebastian whispers hungrily.

"You. *All* of you," I clarify, knowing exactly how he feels.

"Get on your knees, my queen. Show us your appreciation."

A spark of anger shines in her eyes, but I stroke her ass and feel her shudder, so I know Sebastian hit a nerve. She's into this.

# CHAPTER 20
# NEGOTIATIONS
## ARIELLE

"Get on your knees, my queen. Show us your appreciation." I'm a volcano inside. The conversation between Sebastian and Alec melted my brain, and I made sure not to interrupt them as they discussed how they would both be mine.

That was hot as hell—the hottest thing I've ever heard, and so I fall to my knees between them, about ready to give in to anything.

I'm their queen, but from their dangerous looks, I can tell any promise of obedience at court will not apply to our bedroom, and my soul rises to the occasion, yearning to submit to them and see just how good it can feel.

Still...to spite Sebastian, I serve him a nasty grin and inch toward Alec. The sexy royal guard quickly unbuckles his belt and works his stiff cock out of his pants—the only part of his uniform he didn't throw in my face earlier.

His abs strain as he waits not-so-patiently, his fingers digging into his thighs like he's barely holding back from pulling me to him.

Sebastian holds my hair in a fist as I take Alec's length deep in my mouth and pulls just enough for it to drive me wild. I look up at my bodyguard, his face betraying exactly how excited he is to see me like this, on my knees with my hands tied behind my back, sucking his cock in front of my new husband.

I bob my head up and down, licking, sucking, and kissing.

Alec hisses under his breath, his hips moving along with me, his eyes half-mast like he's completely entranced by what I'm doing.

"Fuck, I'm jealous." Sebastian tugs on my hair harder, and I do not resist as he pulls me over to his erection and dart my tongue over the tip, causing him to buck his hips.

I drag my tongue from the base to the tip, denying him what he really wants, teasing him.

Alec steps out of his pants, now naked for my viewing pleasure. He strokes himself up and down slowly, enjoying the show. "She's playing with you."

"I know. Let's make her regret it."

Heat grows in my stomach at how dark and desperate he sounds, and I hold in a whimper when he walks away, craning my neck around to follow him. The way he and Alec stare at each other makes me suspect they're having a quiet conversation. A delicious thrill blazes through my gut, the suspense leaving me wet and hungry.

Alec grips the belt holding my hands behind my back and pulls me to my feet by the leash. The ease with which they have fallen into this still floors me, and I moan when he stretches the fabric of my dress down my cleavage, pinching and pulling roughly at my nipples with one hand until I'm panting, his body pressed flush against my back. He kisses my neck, his hands dipping down the valley between my aching breasts, his long fingers creeping down to the needy space between my thighs, playing me like an instrument as Sebastian watches.

I writhe in his arms, suddenly not feeling so mischievous. Alec ghosts his fingers over my slick folds, the soft caress deliberately maddening.

Sebastian lays over the mattress with a satisfied smirk, his arms braced under his head, his hardness pointed to the ceiling. "She's so beautiful... bring her to me."

Alec flings me on top of him before giving the belt a sharp tug. "Get your gorgeous ass in the air, Lucky."

My core melting from Alec's simple and shameless command, I stretch my ass as far up as I can manage and rest my chin on Sebastian's stomach. The short dress rides up to my hips as I glance up at my husband, his hard cock resting between my breasts. He grabs a fist of my hair again and pushes me down to his erection, his tongue darting out to taste his bottom lip.

Eager to push his buttons, I kiss the v-shape groove above his hip, resisting him. My eyes almost roll inward as Alec kneads my ass with his talented hands and tears my underwear off.

Sebastian stares down at me, his hooded eyes spelling out exactly how annoyed he is with me. "Punish her. Punish her for what she's doing to me."

"I'll make her beg," Alec growls, a promise and a threat all at once. He kneels behind me and gives my drenched folds a slap. I gasp, my mouth opening in surprise. The taste of Sebastian's skin—masculine and salty—invades my senses.

His eyes gleam with lust. "Oh...she's ready for you now."

Alec's cock teases my entrance, sliding across my clit before he gives me half an inch. "Take him inside your mouth, Lucky. Take it all."

I moan and take Sebastian in my mouth, drunk on the taste of him. Just as I relax my jaw enough for Sebastian to hit the back of my throat, Alec enters me in one quick, powerful thrust. My brain short-circuits, a blinding, surprise orgasm ripping through me, making my core so fucking sensitive that I writhe to get away. Alec holds me firmly in place, riding me through it without remorse.

I scream out his name, the sound muffled by Sebastian's cock thrusting deep in my throat.

The flash of heat at their deliciously wicked assault pushes me over the brink of another orgasm, my pleasure flooding around Alec and wrecking the duvet—any question of how much I'm actually enjoying their little stunt *put* to the bedspread, so to speak.

I want more. I'm ravenous for them both. A life with both of them in it, the two of them worshiping me and my body...playing games with my body, it's too good to be true. Especially when they look so at ease with each other, exchanging quips as they argue over the best ways to fuck me.

Alec unties my arms, but instead of granting me freedom, he pulls me up so my back is flush against his chest, his strong and deadly arms caging me in. "What do you want, my queen?"

I struggle to catch my breath, my voice all gruff and commanding as I answer, "I want it all."

Sebastian shifts forward and rolls my breasts in his hands, his red eyes almost black. Alec pecks my shoulder blade, rolling us back until I'm cradled in his lap. I'm so fucking sensitive that even his soft lips feel treacherous and overwhelming as Sebastian peppers kisses along a path down my stomach, heading for my heated core. I squirm to close my knees.

Sebastian chuckles darkly. He grips my thighs, holding them open. "Tut-tut. None of that."

A hot pant falls off my lips, "Wait," but his tongue greedily tests the feel of me.

A gentle hand gathers my hair away from my neck, Alec pulling just enough for it to register. "We want to bite you now, my queen."

My heart stumbles, his husky voice heavy in my ear. Sebastian's fangs nick the tender flesh of my inner thigh at the exact same time, making me feel like a prey, and more excited than I ever thought possible.

Blood is often food to us, but when it comes from another vampire, it's more. It's sacred, giving them a part of me I can't ever get back.

Letting Alec and Sebastian drink from me means I see them as my mates. Eternally.

By Nyx...will they let me drink from them, too?

My mouth waters, my mind flying back to when I had Alec's blood all over me after the attack. I'd never smelled something so...

perfect. Tasting it might just give me a high I'll never recover from, but to hell with caution.

I'm done being reasonable.

"I want you to. Please make me yours. Both of you."

I trust them with my life.

Two pairs of fangs sink into my neck with perfect synchrony, and I groan at the delicious pain of it, my body shaking in response. Alec cradles my neck as he drinks, and Sebastian licks his bloodstained lips. "Hold her steady, Beaumont. I want to come deep inside her with her blood in my mouth."

Alec kisses my neck, blood gliding down the slope toward my shoulder. He holds me closely to him as Sebastian settles between my thighs and enters me.

It's too much, and pleasure radiates off my center to my belly, my chest, my toes as a second orgasm rips through me, a third already building deep beneath the aftershocks of their bites.

Sebastian stares down at Alec and fucks me like he's possessed, like he can taste every gulp the other man is taking from me. Each thrust causes my ass to grind against Alec's cock, my bodyguard feeding from me with gluttony like he's swallowing parts of my soul.

I want to bite them, too, but I'm too busy dying in their arms, being ridden to such oblivion that I forget who I am. Both men don't look like they're very good at sharing, but when it comes to sharing me... they seem to be enjoying the competition, taking turns and switching positions whenever they get too close to release, like they're afraid to be the first to break.

It's more than sex or love or marriage.

Just...better.

# CHAPTER 21

# SALT

## LEO

The flat piece of rock makes twelve jumps before it sinks, and my heart gives a tight squeeze. It's been years since I've thrown rocks at the sea just to pass the time, trying not to think... My legs are submerged to my mid-thigh, the caress of the warm water calming my nerves. The silvery ripples of my throw fade out of view under the watchful eye of the moon. I haven't seen the sea so calm in years, its dark expanse almost as still and inviting as the peace rolling off the creature behind me.

"Interesting dinner," Keenan says, making his presence known though I felt him coming a mile away.

Ever since our first meeting, I can always tell if he's close, like his presence changes the way the air hits my body. It's annoying as fuck.

"They're up in her room working out the *kinks* of their relationship," I joke lightly, trying to appear unfazed.

After Arielle and Alec stormed out of the wedding reception, Sebastian was quick to follow them. I could have joined the trio as they tried to figure out a way to all be together and announce my unwavering intention to stay, but something held me back. No matter how much love and devotion I feel toward Arielle, I'm not a vampire. I'm...held apart.

"But you're here. Alone," he remarks. With his hands hidden inside his jeans, Keenan inches toward me like I'm a wild animal that needs to be tamed. "Do you think she'll work it out with them?"

"Yes. Beaumont can throw all the jealous tantrums he wants... he *loves* her. He couldn't walk away from her if his life depended on it."

*I certainly know the feeling.*

Keenan nods at my analysis. "She's really something. I've rarely known a vampire with such fire and charisma. It's like she was meant to take on the world." Water splashes my knees as he comes to stand next to me. "I could easily fall for her too if I stayed too long."

My gaze snaps to him, the tranquil lull of his powers blown away by his unexpected comment. "Are you thinking of leaving?"

"I don't know. Do ye want me to stay?"

The weight of his gaze suffocates me. It asks too many questions and gives no answers in return. In an instant, I'm crushed by the knee-jerk instinct to ward off the peace threatening to slither inside my cells and snuff out a longing for him I can't quite control.

I avert my gaze and change the subject. "Why are you called angels if you're just another breed of demons?"

"Angels are sometimes seen by our prey. The ones who survive remember us fondly. Angels or demons, none of us come from hell nor heaven. We're a different breed than humans, that's all. The legends say we're all descended from some powerful, dark Gods who once walked the Earth, but I think we're just from different branches on the evolution tree."

I reflect on his answer for a second. "Why do you want to turn me? You said something about me having the right DNA for it and that you knew from the first moment you saw me... How?"

"Supernatural creatures all have an aura around them. A kinetic field, if you will, that sticks to them and can be seen by other demons or humans that have the power to see the invisible."

He moves his hands in front of him like he's merely giving a lecture on mechanics and not trying to explain such an incorporeal thing as magic. "Humans have auras so faint that they remain unseen, and vampire auras are actually pretty dull, too. Yers is... flawless."

I rub the back of my neck, trying to shake off the heat in my gut at how passionate he sounds. How damn perfect he looks under the moon, the line of his jaw straight from Athens' most ancient and beautiful statues.

"Yer aura is a faint tremble of power that lures me in across an entire room, but that's not all. The pain ye feel is like a neon-bright billboard to an angel." He pauses for a moment as though he's searching for the right words. Words that'll bring us closer. "Yer world has spun out of its axis. I know what that feels like. I'll help ye see her safe to her throne, and if by then ye haven't decided to accept my offer, I'll give ye some space to breathe." He licks his full lips, a smile threatening to pierce through his solemn exterior. "But I should warn ye, Leo Callas. As long as I breathe, I'll never stop hunting ye."

My lips quirk at the teasing edge of his voice. "You don't hunt like the vampires I know."

"I'm more patient is all. They hunt for blood and warm bodies, but I..."

I arch a brow, the clear superiority he feels toward vampires not at all a turnoff. If any man can convince me he's better than most bloodsuckers in existence, it's him. "What? You want my soul?" I ask with a grin, not half-serious.

He grips the edge of the rock, his gaze set on the dark horizon. "I want to earn yer trust. I want to see the world through yer eyes and show ye how different it looks from my perspective. Most of all, I need to know who ye are." He tilts his head in my direction ever so slightly. "I want everything yer willing to give, Leo Callas."

It's weird to be wanted so much for doing so little.

"Just because of something in my DNA? Isn't that flawed?"

He chuckles at that, and the tension between us fizzles out into something more comfortable. More honest. "Existence is flawed."

*Ain't that the truth.*

A hot flush rises to my cheeks, and the temptation to lean in and kiss him again short-circuits my rational brain. I love Arielle, and yet, Keenan's magic is undeniable. Even when he mutes himself to allow me to make my own choices, a part of me longs for his peace to engulf everything else. The self-loathing, the doubts, the taboos about desiring another man...

Instead of succumbing to his lure, I stand and peel off my shirt, discarding it on top of the closest rock. "Are you up for a swim?"

He climbs to his feet, too, and grabs the neck of his shirt. The way his eyes dance quickens my pulse. "I thought ye'd never ask."

He snaps off the top button of his jeans, and I jump into the sea not to stare. I swim up to the shallows next to the clutter of rocks that naturally formed where the waves break during a storm and wait for Keenan to catch up. When he emerges barely a foot to my left, my breath stutters. "Damn...Do you have wings or fins?"

He wipes the water away from his eyes. "Wings, but only when it's convenient."

I've been wondering how it works, with his wings being invisible most of the time... are they gone when he doesn't need them, or am I just blind to them?

"Let me see them."

A smirk flickers over his mouth. The water comes up to his waist and licks the hem of his white briefs as his wings blink into view. Long, dark feathers shine like oil under the starry sky, and salted water clings to the ridges in his stomach. A piece of the old me breaks at the sight. There's no shame in longing to be something as beautiful as he is. No shame in giving in.

I'm sure of that, at least.

# CHAPTER 22
# FERAL
ARIELLE

Vampires seldom sleep at night, our metabolisms cranked up in the absence of sunlight. Alec and Sebastian lured me into their embrace after our intense, delicious tryst, and I blink awake with a full moon shining bright in the night sky. My stomach growls, the back of my throat itchy as hell.

Alec stirs next to me. "Fuck, I fell asleep." He rubs his face down, his silvery scars catching the moonlight and creating mesmerizing patterns on his skin.

I slither out of bed and wrap a silk robe around my frame and skitter to the bathroom.

"You must be starving."

"Yes. I'm going to take a quick shower and look for Leo."

The hot water feels amazing, the remnants of our pleasure quickly washed off my body, and I'm left feeling pleasantly clean and satisfied in spite of the growing hunger in my belly.

After patting off the water from my skin and hair, I wrap a robe around my body and return to my men. I open the bathroom door, and in a flash, everything blurs, like the steam from the shower is ten times thicker outside the room. The stench of acid and death assaults my nostrils, and I quickly stop breathing, covering my mouth out of instinct.

*Someone's here.*

Sebastian rolls off the bed, gagging as the smoke starts to clear. The effect of the poisonous vapors turned the veins of his neck and face almost purple, and my chest cramps painfully. On the other side of the bed, the head of a long silver-headed spear buries deep inside Alec's chest.

*No. No no no...*

Agonizing seconds pass, but the weapon must not have reached his heart, because he doesn't dissolve in a cloud of smoke. Doesn't mean he'll live, but it's something.

A sliver of hope.

The assassin's silhouette stalks in the night like a shadow weaving through fog. The vampire possesses the lethal, ninja-like shape of a highly-trained Zhaos soldier. He's wearing black from head to toe, his smaller stature and lightning speed quickening my breath as he slides across the ceramic floor without a sound, his red eyes searching for his mark. I have merely seconds before he recognizes his mistake.

A switch inside me flips.

When Jasper came for me at the hangar, I was too weak to fight. Now, all my newborn vampire muscles ache for violence. I'm not trained, but I'll be damned if I let my men die without raising hell.

Last time, they came in numbers, but this was meant to be a focused one-man operation. If I'd been in that bed next to Sebastian —like I was believed to be—I'd be dead.

The white fog billowing through the air stills as we lock eyes, the centuries of animosity between our clans boiling beneath the surface. A hint of smugness shines through his eyes, his mouth curled in a victorious smile.

Feral as a wounded tiger, I hurl myself at him.

In a blur of speed and power, our bodies collide with a force that could shatter bones, and we both roll to the ground. The attack takes my opponent by surprise, but I realize my own impatience actually put me in jeopardy. In a second, the shadow assassin will reach for one of the weapons strapped to his chest while I'm fighting with my bare hands in a towel...

I spring to my feet and manage to scratch his left eye, a wave of blood pouring out of the wound. Beginner's luck only means that a neophyte will sometimes make an unexpected, different, dumb or even desperate, move. If I'm to die today at the hands of a Zhaos, it won't be running away from this fight.

The assassin quickly pulls out a dagger from his chest rig and draws a sharp circle with his arm, aiming right for my throat. I sidestep, moving quicker than I ever thought possible, and my heart squeezes in my chest.

*Wait...*

Somehow, I saw my opponent's next attack take shape in his head *before* he even moved, and managed to avoid it.

His gloved grip tightens on the hilt of the dagger, and he strikes at my right temple, my brain anticipating his next moves like it knows exactly how and when he's going to react, and I squeeze out of his way again, the sharp blade slicing up the air next to my right ear.

The man's brows pull together, and he switches his dagger to the other hand, obviously frustrated as he tries to stab me again. My tightly-wound body reacts out of instinct, his mind giving away his strategy and allowing me to survive.

Once.

Twice.

Three times.

The blade comes for me time and time again, its owner growing more and more resentful for his failure until we're both gasping for breath.

The whole dance must not have lasted more than a minute, but a minute was enough for Sebastian and Alec to somewhat recuperate from the poison, and my husband roars as he joins in the fight in a blur of limbs, his first instinct to ram into our opponent mirroring my earlier attempt.

Alec sneaks in on the right and kicks the Zhaos off balance. His quick, surgical hit carries the weight of a thousand grudges, the gash in his shoulder oozing blood.

The assassin hits the ground with a loud thud, falling over Sebastian. The red-head vampire wraps himself around our attacker and jabs a knife at his neck.

"Wait! Don't dust him yet." Alec puts his knee over the man's chest to hold him down and tears his sleeve open. A tired groan escapes him as he discards the limp hand back to the ground. "That's not a Zhaos assassin. It's only meant to look like one."

Sebastian beheads him nonetheless. "Zhaos or not, he was good."

A strangled gurgle echoes in from the hallway, and we all barrel outside of the room as Keenan squeezes the life out of a second ninja pretender, the body quickly limp on the stone floor.

Leo stands wide-eyed next to Keenan, both men smelling of sand, salt water, and cheap beer, like they just returned from the beach. "Are you okay?"

I blush a deep shade of red and nod, wondering if he came by my room after we cut the wedding reception short. If he heard us...

Alec rolls the bloody corpse over to its back, and recognition flashes in his eyes as he observes the second dead assassin. "I know him. He was a widow maker, too. A mercenary. One of the best."

Sebastian rubs down his tired face. "It means whoever hired them is still alive. Widow makers always finish their job, but only as long as the one who called the hit is still inclined to pay."

"It confirms our theory that Jasper wasn't working alone," I whisper under my breath, squeezing Sebastian's hand as he struggles to breathe through the pain. "But who sent them? Peter or Garrett?"

"Or both." Keenan offers with a sad smile.

Sebastian slips on his jeans before sitting on the bed. "No... if

Garrett, Peter, and Jasper were all working together, there wouldn't be a need for games and pretenses. The secrecy, the convoluted moves... it means whoever is working against us still needs to keep up appearances."

"Peter was sleeping with Victor, so I'd say Garrett is the most likely culprit," I say quickly, hoping he'll understand the need to air out his father's secrets.

Alec grits his teeth together. "I agree."

Leo scratches the back of his neck. "But the assassin seemed to want to spare Sebastian... that's a vote for Peter."

I bite my bottom lip, my hands shaking. "We need to gather all the important players together in one room and let me figure out the truth."

"I'll call Peter and tell him I have important information concerning Jasper's death and the Pereiras. Ask him for a private audience with both him and your brother. Then, we can figure out which of them wants us dead. We need to act fast, or another wave of mercenaries will hit us soon, and there are only so many close-calls we can have before they manage to kill us."

"That's not a bad idea. We were supposed to leave this evening, but I say we move out now."

Alec stretches out his healed shoulder, nodding at Sebastian's suggestion. He meets all our gazes in turn, his dark, commanding stare scattering goosebumps on my neck. "No outsiders. The five of us, only. Until we've unmasked our enemy and gotten rid of the hit on the queen, we're all that we have."

# CHAPTER 23
# HOMECOMING
## ALEC

The Delacroix estate is well guarded, so our approach is carefully planned. Arielle wants to control the narrative and get a chance to test her court's loyalties before making a formal appearance. We certainly won't give her enemies a chance to stab her in the back, and so we planned to arrive right before sunrise.

Fog licks the ground, the large cluster of trees near the secret entrance to the underground tunnels half hidden in a vaporous gray cloud. The grass swishes under our boots as we enter the silent, wooded area, the unbeaten path hard to follow in the murky dawn.

A blood-red pantsuit hugs the queen's delicious curves, her dark hair braided to one side, her lipstick a little messy from the unbridled kiss we shared on the plane. A black, hooded cape covers her slender form and matches Sebastian's. Both royals blend with the shadows a few feet behind me, Leo and Keenan closing the march behind them.

"Dammit, Beaumont. How can you navigate through this fog? I can barely see my feet."

"I've got a good sense of direction. Better instinct. *Eyes*," I crack.

He skips forward to fall in step with me. "Are you implying you're better than me?"

"Yes."

Our new king consort keeps cracking jokes about returning from his honeymoon, and I'm tempted to laugh at a few of them, his larger than life personality a constant source of entertainment.

My royal guard uniform molds to my body, the significance of our homecoming not lost on me. As we reach the secret door blocking the entrance to the catacombs, I motion for Keenan and Leo to keep watch and approach the door below the rocky face of the hill alone.

"Qui va là?" A voice calls from the other side of the door.

"Alec Beaumont. Open up, soldier."

The secret entrance to the tunnels cracks open, and obvious relief warms the young guard's face. "We're happy to see you, Sir. With Jasper gone and the king dead, we received conflicting orders from the Prime Minister and Master of War. We're not sure who's in charge anymore."

I stare at him as though he's lost his mind, trying to imprint on his colleague exactly how stupid his sentence was. "What the fuck are you talking about? Who's the highest-ranking officer on the scene?"

His mouth opens and closes before he stutters, "Y-You are, Sir."

"Exactly. You four, go and fetch me both the Prime Minister and the Master of War. I don't care if they're sleeping. Tell them to come at once, and escort them straight to the crypt, no matter what they say. Don't wake anyone else, and don't allow them to delay." I meet the eyes of another guard, his face familiar enough for me to feel at ease even if I can't remember his name. "And you, call for the guard to secure the royal crypt. No one else is allowed in or out until I say so."

The new recruit hangs back awkwardly, delaying the departure of his comrades with his hesitation. "But Sir, the queen has asked to be alerted of all daytime arrivals."

The four guards behind him exchange a glance like they're confused about the chain of command again.

"The *dowager*-queen is not—" I start, annoyed by his reluctance to follow my orders.

Arielle removes the hood of her cape, and the ambivalent soldiers' eyes immediately widen. "Get her, too. Peter, Adele, and Garrett."

I open my mouth to speak, but she places a gentle hand on my wrist to stop me. She sizes the recruit up and down with a serious, imperial gaze. "Go now, soldier."

The guard bows with an arm braced to his chest, his spine straight as an arrow. "At once, my queen."

I rub down my jaw, feeling exhausted by all these schemes already. *Jesus, I hate politics.* "We have all our pieces. We just need to figure out which ones are against us."

*"We'll let them see each other, then ask to speak to one of them alone. If two of them are involved, they might get paranoid and turn on each other. Once we figure out who screwed us, the innocent ones will act as witness as we secure the fate of the traitor."* Arielle explains telepathically.

Peter, Garrett, and Adele soon join us by the entrance of the royal chapel. Garrett is all disheveled, looking like he was pulled right out of bed, while Peter's brown hair is perfectly slicked over his head.

Adele's eyes are red, her skin ashen, her round belly the only thing about her that doesn't look brittle and defeated.

"Ari!" she cries out, running to the queen for a hug.

The women embrace each other, tears glazing their closed lids.

'What's going on?" Garrett asks, walking up the aisle, his gaze bouncing from me to the queen for an explanation, and for the first time since I killed the faux-Jasper, I dare to hope that my older brother hasn't been the one pulling the strings.

*"What do you think?"* Arielle asks into my mind.

The dread at the pit of my stomach pulses. *"Peter first."*

She nods discreetly. "I have important information to share with all of you, but before I do, I need a few answers." She turns, and asks, "Peter. Can we see you first?"

Sebastian squints at his father. The two men look more alike than not as they size each other up, both of them silent until the thick door of the chapel closes behind us. Leo and Keenan guard the door while Arielle and Sebastian walk toward the stone altar, and I stand between them and Peter in case the Prime Minister decides to solve this disagreement with violence—but my instincts are quiet, and I suspect the old vampire knows better than to use his fists in a situation like this.

"Am I suspected of some crime? This feels awfully like an interrogation." Peter's eyes narrow at his son, the grim curve of his mouth spelling out his disappointment. "I was awfully sorry to hear I'd missed your wedding."

Sebastian squeezes Arielle's hand, his eyes flashing with anger, the sordid vibes of their decade-long feud exposed for everybody else to see. "We were too eager to wait. After what you tried to pull with Pereira, it was only fair to make it official quickly. Before you schemed to keep her away from me."

He ignores his son's biting comments and turns to Arielle. "Were you worried that I would vote for my grandson instead of you? Marrying my good-for-nothing son sure sounds like an overreaction on your part, Your Grace."

The queen's jaw clenches, and she looks down at the Prime Minister with contempt. "I won't allow you to talk to me like that, not if you want to keep your job."

*Or your head...*

Peter cracks up at her guile, his gaze unwavering. "Seems you're the one whose fate is unclear."

"Stop bluffing, daddy dearest. You might hate me, but I'm your only son." He wraps an arm around the queen's waist, the possessive gesture not as jarring as it would have been just a day ago. "The children *we* have together will be royal."

"Speak plainly, son. No more games."

139

"Rumors have it Adele was sleeping with someone else..." Sebastian trails off. "Who knows who her children's father is, really?"

Peter's brows pull together, his top lip curled in an expression of disgust for a fleeting moment before the mask of the careful politician returns. "You think I didn't check? Human DNA testing has only existed for a few decades, but the supernatural world has always had efficient, reliable ways to determine parentage. The boy is Victor's son."

Arielle meets his gaze head on. "I'm to be crowned queen, Peter. I'm the rightful heir."

"You are. I see that now."

"Then we don't disagree. I'm glad." She gives me the signal that means she thinks he's saying the truth, and I relax my stance a smidge. Damn...if Peter is not lying, then my brother and his lover... I swallow hard.

Peter risks a glance in my direction. "What now?"

"Leo, let Adele in, please," Arielle says with her lips curled down.

Sebastian grits his teeth together, his agitation palpable.

I think, on some level, we'd all hoped it'd be Peter.

## CHAPTER 24
# THRONE OF SHADOWS
## ARIELLE

T he lights of the chapels' chandelier flicker in the breeze as Leo opens the thick doors to retrieve our next guest. Peter Chastain wraps a hand over the ornate back support of the pew and bites his bottom lip. I follow his every move, still unsure about him. His thoughts are like sand, slipping through my fingers as I try desperately to make sense of his inner musings. He did plan to overthrow me before, and he's livid that Sebastian defied him, but his keen mind is quickly going through the pros and cons of each scenario, calculating his odds to remain in power.

*"90% of regents destabilize reigns, and 23% are murdered in the first year, but too many men have the princess' ear already. And Sebastian will do everything in his power to humiliate me..."* he thinks.

I leave him to his statistics and concentrate on Adele. She walks into the room, holding her pregnant belly, and I watch her father's reaction.

*"Poor sweetheart, they could have let her be. It's not like she has any political insight, and she's so close to labor."*

I press my lips together. Unless Peter knows I can read his

conscious thoughts, he's not scheming with his daughter to murder me, that's for sure.

"Adele, welcome," I say quickly, knowing I let the silence run a little long.

Her gaze flies from her father's pout to each of my men. "What's going on, Ari? Why did you wake us up at this hour? Is there trouble?" She walks up the aisle but stops a few paces before she reaches her father near the front row.

"Yes. A band of mercenaries has been following me for weeks, ever since my Nightfall. We thought they were assassins sent by the Zhaos, but new information implies they've been hired from within this court."

The bloody tears in her red eyes are gone, and her face slowly wrinkles into a desperate scowl. "Will it never end? First Ludovic, then Victor, then you..." she chokes up and hides her disgruntled face in her palms.

*"When you're dead, I will finally be free to rule this court as I see fit."*

The last part catches me by surprise, and my mouth opens on a silent gasp.

By Nyx...it makes sense.

Why would she be crying? Why would she mourn her husband when she was so clearly not in love with him? She's just faking it. When we summoned her, she genuinely looked like she'd been crying her eyes out for hours...

My eyes fly to Alec, my brain still trying to put the puzzle together as I warn him. *"It's her."*

But before my royal guard can even acknowledge my revelation, the air blurs, and when I find Adele again, her arm is wrapped around Leo's throat near the exit. Her voice has completely changed, sharp as glass as she says, "How did you know?"

My pulse grows cold at the sight of her long red nails sinking inside the tender flesh of my first-blood. "Stop!"

"Nobody moves, or he's dead."

There's no doubt that she will kill Leo if any of us try anything. A big part of me is screaming that she will kill him regardless, her mind like an endless well of bitterness.

*"They killed him. Killed my love just like that. I should tear out their hearts and feed them to my little one. I'm going to make them all pay."* She tightens her hold around Leo's neck. "I saw it in your eyes, just then. You knew I was lying."

"Yes," I admit, trying to buy time.

A joyless sneer deforms her face. "I guess you of all people should understand what it feels like to be used by the men in your life, but it doesn't give you a free pass. Your family has always been the problem. As long as one Delacroix remains in this world, it will never change. When you're all dead, I will put a new regime in place. Vampires should live for themselves. We've got rules to protect the humans, rules to protect the endangered demon species... Where are the rules for *us*? For our children? We're better than humans and other demons. We should be free to do what we want and not answer to anyone." Her eyes fall to Leo's neck. "Like him, for example. You clearly care for him more than you should, but what is he, really? Just a body for us to enjoy, and there's enough of them now for us not to be so fucking careful with our food. That's all humans will ever be." She flashes her fangs and leans toward Leo's artery. If she tears into the carotid, he'll die in less than a minute.

And I will be powerless to stop it.

"Let him go!" I scurry down the altar only to freeze in place near Alec. Leo's blood perfumes the air, small trickles of red gliding down from every nick Adele made with her nails. Alec digs the balls of his feet into the ground, but before he moves, Keenan clears his throat.

Up until this point, the angel had muted his powers almost completely. Peter hadn't even glanced twice at him when he'd entered the chapel, probably assuming he was under Alec's command. Adele hadn't asked about him, either.

I expect him to blink behind Adele and take advantage of her surprise to try and save Leo's life. Instead, the angel engulfs the room in his magic, and a unstoppable sense of peace rams into me like a tsunami, my balled fists falling at my sides.

A bright, golden halo shines above his chestnut curls, and enormous black wings sprout from his back, tearing through his shirt. His skin gleams from within, almost blinding, as though we're staring directly into a forbidden piece of heaven.

*So beautiful...*

Alec, Peter, Sebastian and I... we're all staring at him.

Adele, too.

He approaches her with a sad smile, his brows raised with compassion. "You've been unhappy, luv."

"I have." She says slowly, her entire body trembling.

"You don't have to carry it alone, ye know."

Her voice breaks with a thousand different cracks. It brims with a bottomless sorrow that bares every broken part of her blackened soul. "Who are you?"

"I'm here for you, luv. Come to me."

I hold my breath as she obeys, inching toward the angel with small steps, leaving Leo behind like she doesn't even remember he's there.

Keenan gathers her in his arms and tucks a loose strand of hair behind her ear. "What about the third fellow..." Keenan trails off, not breaking eye contact with her.

"Garrett," I clarify. Alec meets my gaze, and I give him an encouraging nod.

"Tell me, luv. Was Garrett involved in your plans to kill the queen?"

I invade Adele's mind once more, but her thoughts are too fragmented for me to make sense of them.

She gives a small, cooing sound, and her lids drop like she wants to curl into Keenan's embrace and sleep there forever. "No."

"Who's the father of yer unborn child?"

"Jasper is the father." She chokes up, her head nestled in Keenan's chest. "But he's dead. They killed him." Tears stream down her face, red streaks quickly coloring her alabaster cheeks.

The golden glow bathing the room dims, and sweat shines over the angel's brow as he pats the woman's back in a soothing manner. "There. You can rest now."

I swallow hard, the weight of the last few minutes crashing into me, my muscles sore despite the non-violent resolution. For a moment, I wish I was the one cocooned in Keenan's magic, feeling nothing but peace.

A splash of weirdly scented water splashes at her feet, and Adele presses her lips tight together, a strangled growl popping out of her clenched jaw. The strange magic that was pacifying her wavers, Keenan's golden-white aura fading even more.

"Fuck... She's in labor." Sebastian grinds out, his face whiter than the roses decorating the altar.

"Now?"

"Yes, now. Go and wake the doctor," he orders Leo, my first-blood standing stock-still by the door.

"It's a trick," Peter hisses under his breath.

Alec squints at the pool of liquid on the stones, his nostrils flaring. "I don't think so."

My husband zooms over to his sister and grabs her hand, ushering her to the top of the stairs. Alec is quick on his heels, both men taking hold of one arm.

Leo hurries out, and Garrett enters the room, the haze of sleep gone from his demeanor. "What's going on?"

"Adele Chastain is an enemy of the crown. Her and Jasper plotted to have Victor killed and tried to murder the queen."

I expect the oldest Beaumont to ask questions or argue, but he lets out a small, "Fuck," before his expression turns serious and analytical. "What should we do?"

"Gather the queen's servants and Jasper's. Some of them might have been involved. Initiate a complete lockdown and tell the soldiers to double their vigilance. No one is to be let in or out without the queen's express authorization. The royal guard should search Adele's rooms for evidence."

The two men have it all under control, so I take my place at Sebastian's side, knowing how heart-wrenching the whole situation must be for him.

"The doctor is on his way, just...try to relax," Sebastian says to his sister, and I give his hand an encouraging squeeze. He knew his family was fucked up, but not to this extent...

The doctor comes rushing in and barks a few orders at Peter and Sebastian. They relocate Adele to the floor and the physician takes his place between her legs.

The pregnant vampire is shaken by contractions every few seconds. Blood and sweat stick to her black hair, her arms shaking. "Which one of you killed him? Was it you?" she asks, the remnants of Keenan's magic gone from her voice, the pain coming in quick waves close together.

Sebastian shakes his head. "No."

The dowager queen closes her eyes, tears spilling over her closed lids. "Then who did it?"

"I did," I lie, knowing I shouldn't let anyone else take the blame for something I would have done if I was given the opportunity.

Adele snarls. "Felipe Pereira wants your head. You'll be lucky to last a month. How did you get rid of the necklace?"

My pulse flutters at my neck, her disappointment tangible. "So... you're the one who had the necklace made?"

She clams shut, but I can see that I'm right. As the queen, she had access to the court's warlocks. Jasper didn't.

"Pereira will pay for his sins," I add solemnly, the memories of the burns still hot around my throat.

Peter grimaces, looking particularly displeased. "My Queen, we have to smooth things over with Pereira. We can't afford to have both him and the Zhaos after us."

I fail to mask the outrage and disbelief in my voice. "Thank you, Peter. I'll take that under advisement."

"I meant no disrespect—"

"Your daughter is giving birth. Concentrate on that." If this woman hadn't just tried to kill Leo and admitted to plotting various ways to kill or enslave me, I would order the bastard to leave.

But from where I'm sitting, those two deserve each other. Peter molded Adele into the monster she became without realizing it, and I need him to take a good look at his creation.

He kneels next to Adele and grips her hand, his mouth curled down in a mix of horror and disappointment. "Why would you try and destroy everything I have worked for?"

She chuckles like she's lost her mind. "Why? Oh, I don't know. What about the fact that you were fucking my husband? Or that we both couldn't stand the other's touch, and yet I had to sleep with him every fertile cycle so you would have an heir. I wish the assassin we sent after him had killed you too, like he was supposed to."

Her bitter rambles turn into a symphony of groans and cries. The doctor calmly encourages her to push, that she's close to release... I'm powerless to look away, wishing everything was different.

I thought of Adele as a friend, an ally, a sister...

A minute later, the screams of the bloodling engulf the room, and we all stand stock still. Under our frozen stares, Alec and Sebastian's nephew is born.

# CHAPTER 25
# SENTENCE
## ARIELLE

Fragrant blood spices up the air of the throne room. As every vampire well knows, traitors' blood smells sweetest of all. Of course, most would consider it barbaric to paint your halls with the blood of your enemies, but not us. No matter how civilized vampires become, we understand blood above all else. The demons that die under the law endanger our way of life, and yet the way justice is dispensed in this kingdom leaves a lot to be desired.

The Delacroix sigil burns on the wall behind my throne, a constant reminder of the damage my brothers did to our kingdom. Blood taints. Fire purifies.

I plan to be a fire for the ages.

A week has passed since the birth of Adele's son, and it's both fitting and ghoulish that my first tribunal after my coronation should be centered on her trial. She's been under strict guard ever since, her complete testimony taken in by the investigators and warlocks responsible for the inquiry, the depths of her betrayal unequaled.

Jasper was mostly just her lover but also her puppet as she used her name and connections to orchestrate the whole thing. She now has to answer for all those crimes in front of the court.

"Adele Chastain you stand here accused of the murder of our late king, your late husband Victor Delacroix. You conspired with Jasper Beaumont, your lover and the father of your child, to kill the king and myself to seize power. You hired assassins made to look like our enemies to disperse blame, and you ordered them to kill your own father, the current Prime Minister."

The proof of her pregnancy is gone, her pixie shape back, making her look small. Almost childlike. If I hadn't read her dark, compassionless thoughts myself, I could never believe the depths of her wickedness.

"Do you have something to say in your defense?" I ask loudly.

She cracks a wry smile. "Shouldn't you be on my side? Can't you imagine how it felt, to be cast aside and overlooked, forced to live a life I didn't want? Don't you have any pity at all?"

After I confessed to killing Jasper, Adele cursed me to the nine hells. I didn't expect her to appeal to our similarities. I raise my chin, the royal mask fully in place. "Don't pretend we're the same. You schemed to condemn me to the same fate as you. You convinced Victor to get rid of me, and when that failed, you tried to kill me." I pause to add some gravitas to my next announcement. "There's only one possible sentence for a treason of this magnitude, and that sentence is death."

Peter's gaze bounces to the ground for a split second. I hope he feels guilty for what he did to his daughter, but I can't pardon her or reduce the gravity of her sentence.

Adele's mouth opens in a mix of surprise and disgust, and I get the impression she truly believed she'd get away with her sins. "Eleanor killed your other brother, and she still lives."

"Again... I fear you mistake me for a fool if you think I view your crimes in the same light."

Whatever Adele says, she didn't kill Victor to get herself out of a bad marriage, in self-defense, or because he was abusive to her. She killed him to seize power. If Peter forced her to marry him, that's a pity, but she showed her true colors when she had that necklace made under false pretenses by the court's warlocks.

The law should have the final word in a matter like this, not my anger or my ego. And in Adele's case, the law offers no wiggle room at all.

I clench my jaw, my resolve clear and unwavering. "Do you have any last wishes?"

The room grows somber, Sebastian's face a shade whiter than it was a minute ago, but I read nothing but regretful acceptance in the bunch of his features. Peter too.

Alec scowls from the side, about ready to carry out the sentence himself. I named him head of the royal guard, and his friend Jude is sitting next to him. The taciturn guard is about to receive a promotion for his loyalty and the part he played in getting me out of Brazil. After this trial, I have less depressing matters to address, starting with my intention to partner with Keenan and his angels to bring peace back to the western continent.

This trial is wretched.

Condemning Adele to death, the girl I've known since I was born, isn't easy. It's certainly not fun. But I do believe it's necessary. Sebastian wasn't wrong when he asked me if I was cruel enough to reign. The Shadow World doesn't deal well in shades of gray, and if I'm to rule over the demons that roam the continent and reform the court, I need to show strength and clarity.

"Adele Chastain was our queen. As such she let down the entire court, and our people. Countless people have died because of her schemes, and who knows how many more will suffer because of it. I condemn her to death, as is prescribed by our laws. Does anyone here have something to say in her defense?"

Silence moves through the room, the other vampires present not moving or breathing. The crowd is immobile, as only a vampire crowd can be, making this silence the most complete silence of all. And that comforts me for the decision I made.

Adele wanted to destroy everything. I can never let myself forget how her unhappiness drove her to hatred. I can't help but acknowledge the reasons for her crimes.

"Adele, now, you have the opportunity to voice the reasons for your betrayal to this court. If you wish to proceed, I'll have the warlocks bind you to the truth, so nobody here can doubt the truth in your testimony."

I'm offering her a chance to pull the veil off her father's crimes and drag him along with her to ruin. Sebastian and I talked about it, and he's on board.

The court can't change with Peter Chastain at the helm, and yet I can't overlook his pull with the government. Hopefully, Adele takes her chance to dismantle the aura of righteousness he catered around himself.

But who does she hate more? Me, for being so close to living the life she always wanted? Or Peter, for ruining hers in the first place? I guess it doesn't matter. It certainly won't change the fact that she'll be dead before the night is over, and I will have to live with her death on my conscience.

My first true hard decision as Queen, and I expect it'll stay with me forever.

# CHAPTER 26
# WINGS
## LEO

"Ari," I whisper quietly after entering the bedroom, trying to wake her without a start. "The government is ready to render its decision concerning Peter."

Alec pecks her on the lips and rolls off their bed. "I'll get dressed and meet you outside in the gardens."

Sebastian stretches like a cat, the redheaded vampire naked in the moonlight. "Jury's out...that didn't take long."

Arielle wraps a robe around her naked frame and hurries off to her closet to get dressed. "Do you think it's a good sign?"

"Could be." He shrugs like the fate of his father doesn't affect him, but I don't think he's fooling anyone.

Alec and Arielle hustle out as soon as they're decent, and I'm left with Sebastian, the vampire's mouth curled in a scowl of regret... or indecision.

"You don't have to go, you know. They can deal with this between them."

"I know." He slips on a pair of jeans. "What's your father like, Leo?"

I fail to mask a cringe at the direction this conversation is taking. "My father died a long, long time ago."

"Oh. I'm sorry."

"Don't be. He was every bit of a disappointment, too. Blamed my mother and myself for stealing his dreams."

He fastens the buttons of his shirt and straightens the collar, quiet for a moment. "You understand, then," he finally says, his voice cracking at the end.

"I do." My gaze flicks to the ground. "What will happen to the baby, now?" I ask, thinking about the poor little one who became an orphan this week.

"We'll raise him here, under our care. Alec and I already made the necessary arrangements. He won't have a father or a mother, but he'll have two uncles that'll strive to be better fathers than either of us have had. And Arielle will love the child, despite the sins of his parents," Sebastian declares with passion, no longer fighting to appear unperturbed.

The emotion on his breath throws me for a loop. "He'll be lucky, then," I whisper.

Sebastian's gaze flicks to my neck, but before I can move, he shakes his head and clears his throat. "Hum. Do you know where my first-blood, Fred, is?"

"I think she's in her room, my lord."

He nods emphatically at that and pats my shoulder. "Thank you, Leo."

I lick my lips, wondering if I imagined the hunger in his eyes and what to make of it.

Sebastian slows down near the threshold and turns back to look at me. "I know you're not exactly comfortable with the arrangement, so I won't push. But just so we're clear, I'm interested. Hell, Beaumont is interested, too. He's just a bit more old fashioned about these things. And Arielle would never dare ask you, but a foursome would drive her wild."

I chuckle at his honesty. "You want to drink my blood?"

"Hell, yes. But like I said, I won't push. Blood. Me watching the two of you as she feeds. A foursome. Any combination imaginable or nothing at all. Whatever you want. You're the boss."

Somehow, he doesn't make my skin crawl. Sebastian doesn't look at me like I'm a piece of meat. He doesn't speak as though I'm below him or different, but more conversationally... like a friend telling me all about the shiny new stock he invested in, letting me in on the opportunity of a lifetime.

It doesn't change my perspective, exactly, but it's not all bad. I could get on board with it if it wasn't for the helplessness I felt in the chapel, when Adele had her claws in my neck.

I double-back and wait for Arielle to come out of the session.

"Where is Sebastian?"

"He decided not to come along." I wrap my arms around her, the chill of the night scattering goosebumps along her arms. "They decided against his father, yes?"

"He's relieved of his position, effective immediately. Sadly, he hasn't broken any laws, but he's lost most of his gravitas, at least." She shivers and holds me close, her lids fluttering shut at the heat. A content sigh falls past her lips. "Look at the moon."

I meet her hungry gaze, tempted to flatten her to the trellis and find out exactly how thirsty she is. My belly tightens at the thought, the gardens silent and perfect for a late night tryst under the moonlight...

I wince regretfully. "I think you should go and talk to him. He seemed upset, earlier. I think he's looking for...bloody distractions."

She observes me closely, her lips tucked between her teeth. "Leo...Did Sebastian ask to bite you? Because I'd never demand to share you with him. Never."

"I know you wouldn't." I kiss her hard, desperate for an additional moment of intimacy between us before I tell her what's been on my mind since we returned.

She runs her tongue over my jugular.

"I'm sorry, Ari. I've been blaming you for a decision I made, for a system you had no true part of, and denied you some common decency. I held myself away from you, and that's entirely my fault."

"You don't have to—I..." she bites her bottom lip, so perfect under the silvery sky that my heart aches with her beauty. "Thank you, Leo. That means a lot."

I cup her face, pulling her closer, her tantalizing lips beckoning me closer. "I love you, Arielle Beatrice Delacroix."

"I love you too, Leo Callas."

We kiss in the secluded gardens, and I know everything will be alright.

"I should go and speak with Sebastian now. I'll see you inside, yes?"

I lick my lips. Here goes...

"Before you go, there's something I've been meaning to talk to you about." A small chuckle escapes me as I link our fingers, trying to soften my words. "God, I sound so serious..." I meet her gaze again. "I love you, Arielle. And I hate that Adele used me against you. She knew I was the weakest link, the easy mark. If Keenan hadn't been there...I'd be dead, or she would have used me to escape. If I stay here with you, and love you the way I want to, others will try to take advantage of that. It'll make me a target." I scratch the back of my neck, what I have to do becoming clearer with each sentence. "If I dare to hope for a life alongside you, things have to change."

The clouds obscure the moon, her eyes now draped in shadows. "What do you mean?"

"*You* might learn to see me as more than a human, more than a meal on two legs, but you'll always be a vampire. But your court won't see me as more than a human. Your enemies will be able to kill me with one finger. I'll age... But that's not all of it. Those are all good, rational excuses." My gaze glued to the sky, the throng of questions and doubts comes to a halt in my overactive brain. The events of the last few weeks still for a moment, enough for me to see through the storm clearly. "As long as I'm mortal, we won't be on equal footing. And I'm not talking about wealth or power... *That* I could get used to. But we're different species, Arielle. You're smart, strong, and almost immortal. You intend to use your powers for good—like Keenan and that witch who saved you. It makes me think I can do the same. I want to be...more."

She licks her lips slowly, her brows bent in question. "You want to become a vampire?"

My nose wrinkles, and I grab her hands in mine, hoping I can convey just how important her blessing is to me. "No. I'm sorry if that wasn't clear. Keenan is offering to make me like him. I want to say yes."

"After it's done, you and I will be equals—-maybe not in status, since you'll be Queen, but in spirit. In knowledge. There's so much I don't know, Arielle, and if you teach me, if I don't get a chance to discover how I fit in this world by myself, I fear I'll never feel like I truly belong, outside of you."

She holds me closer, taking refuge in my arms. "I understand."

And I'm so fucking relieved to hear it, I could cry.

Maybe it's enough to be a human in this world, but to be the man she needs, the man she deserves, I need to be on her level. And I love her even more for supporting my decision.

KEENAN DOESN'T SEEM surprised to see me when I join him in his room. The angel has announced his intention to leave tomorrow, and the slight smirk at the corner of his mouth tells me he knew I wouldn't let him leave without saying goodbye. His bag is packed at the foot of the bed, ready to go.

"I still have questions," I announce, not beating around the bush.

"How did you know it would work, with Adele I mean? If you're this powerful, why didn't you just use your powers on Jasper and his minions back in the hangar? Why fight at all if you can avoid it?"

He smiles like I'm still not asking the right questions. "The more broken someone is, the more they crave peace. And besides...I can't seduce an entire army."

"Broken... is that what I am?" I told Arielle I was ready to hear Keenan out, but inside, I'm both excited and terrified. What if I'm jumping too fast into this?

Keenan seems to be following my train of thought, and he sobers up immediately, the teasing edge of his voice gone. "Remember how you felt when we first met? How a part of you craved death?" He pauses for a second before adding, "Adele had sunk a thousand leagues deeper than you ever did."

I can't imagine her pain, and while she certainly deserved her ending, I'm glad her father was held responsible for his part, too.

"I changed my mind. I want to know more about angels." I wince at how dishonest I sounded... fuck it. "I want to become like you. I love her, but I can't be a meal on two legs."

"She might resent you for it." He considers me with an impassive face, his reaction——or lack thereof—quickening my pulse.

"I don't care. I need to be more for her, or I won't be able to protect her. How do we do it?"

A small smile twists his lips. "So eager... Did you guys have a fight? Are you angry?"

"No."

"Lonely, then? Are you jealous of her vampires?"

"No."

The suspicious arch of his brows melts, and he nods like he finally believes me. "It'll take months before you can control your new powers. You'll have to come to the US with me, and meet the others. When you're ready, we can come back here, and vampires and angels can truly work together to change the world for the better."

The stiffness in my spine eases. "Okay."

"And ye'll need to feed on humans, too. Even though angels can eat food, you can't kid yourself into believing you won't crave blood. Or that you could learn to live without it."

"I figured."

"And you won't be as strong as me for a long, long while."

It's my turn to frown, my arms almost shaking from the doubt in his tone. "Are you trying to talk me out of this?"

He takes a deep breath in, his chest heaving under his white cotton shirt, this mountain of a man finally crumbling in front of me. "Not at all," he whispers, and the sound is husky, intimate.

I blush crimson at the tenderness in his eyes.

"Leo...I dreamed of this moment, yearned for it even. Do you know how long it's been since I turned someone like you? Someone who has the right DNA to become a true sire?"

"A sire?"

"Yes. I believe that, with time, you will become as powerful as I am, Leo. A sire is an angel who can create others with his venom."

My mouth dries up. "Are there many?"

His eyes dim, now almost gray instead of blue. "I'm the last one, actually."

My breath catches in my throat at the weight of his revelation. "It must be so lonely..."

He offers me a small smile. "It is."

"Am I interrupting something?" Arielle's tone is curious as she tiptoes inside the room with her arms linked at her back, and yet a tinge of worry dances in her piercing gaze.

"Ye should tell her of our plans before we proceed." Keenan's lips curl in the shadow of a smile. "But I do hope she won't change yer mind."

"I did talk to her. She supports my decision."

Keenan smiles, his whole demeanor changed by my admission. His clouded eyes brim with joy as he looks between the both of us. Joy and something else. Something...darker. "Ye do?"

"Yes, but I have questions, too."

My cheeks flush even more at the knowledge that she eaves-dropped on our discussion as Keenan waves her over.

His gaze travels between us, and he scratches the angle of his jaw with his lips slightly parted, as though an important idea just occurred to him. "I know ye're not exactly looking forward to feeding on humans, Leo, but to transition, ye have to drink blood until yer prey is near death."

Arielle slips her hand into mine, and my heartbeats finally settle down. "I figured...*near* death, though? Not dead?" I've got the feeling he's easing me in, his mouth tensed at the corners.

"I sure hope not. Ye see, Leo, vampires like Arielle transition when they drink human blood. But to catch my disease, ye're going to feed from me."

"But I thought—" my brows pull together. "You?"

"Aye. Almost all of me."

My mouth dries up, a searing heat invading my stomach at the thought of drinking from Keenan's neck...

"The process will make me very weak. I need someone there to oversee the process and restrain ye if ye lose control. I usually have another angel doing it, but I can make an exception. Just this once." He drops his gaze to his feet, suddenly looking shy and uncertain. "If our queen wants to help ye through the transition."

"I'm still a newborn, how do you know I won't lose my head?" Arielle asks quietly.

"I trust ye, Your Highness. Besides...I think yer presence could make the process more pleasant for me. Maybe with yer magic, the bite doesn't have to be so painful."

"I'm not sure..." I don't know what I expected, but I didn't think it would involve Ari, of all people. I don't want to accidentally hurt her in a ritual that Keenan describes as a very volatile situation.

She gives my hand a good tug, turning me to her. "Let me be the one who sees you safely into your new life."

"Alright," I breathe against her lips.

Keenan pulls his shirt off his body and sits on the plush sofa. I grin at Arielle, the lovely vampire staring at the ridges in his stomach with a tinge of guilt, her fingers cold in mine.

Our gazes meet over Keenan's shoulder. "Ready?" she asks, almost taunting me into action. "I'll help you out a little. Human teeth aren't exactly engineered for this."

I nod and inch closer to her and Keenan, my heart about to jump out of my chest. Last chance to turn back, and yet I can't bring myself to fear the monster I'm about to become. I'm...excited.

Arielle uses her venom to coat the tender skin of Keenan's neck, and his gaze immediately glazes over. He groans as her magic starts to flow through his veins, and I know exactly how he's feeling. Lucky bastard.

She nicks his jugular open until blood trickles out of the wound, humming under her breath before she moves out of the way. A hint of red colors her lips as she smiles, and Keenan pulls her in his lap for a kiss while I work out my nerves and lean down to taste his blood. Without giving myself the time to agonize over my choice, I press my mouth to the gash and swallow a mouthful of blood.

I expect it to taste like my own—metallic and bitter—but the rich liquid is actually sweet and enticing. It's eerie and wild to be drinking him for a change, and a suffocating thrill shoots up my spine. Keenan's blood doesn't compare to anything I've ever tasted.

My tongue darts out, and I hold him closer, biting down on the wound for better access, sucking down his life essence like it's the very air I need to survive.

Keenan's blood is now my oxygen, and I need it more than I could ever need food or water.

I feel unmade.

Desperate.

Ravenous.

I gasp out for him, each gulp of blood rearranging my soul into something more. Something ancient and powerful and different. Keenan caresses the back of my neck and lets out a small, needy sigh like he wants to give me all there is to give, and I take and take from him without restraint.

I drink from him until my lungs and stomach feel full and needier still, the pleasure of each mouthful only eclipsed by the bliss of the next, my legs and arms stronger and more flexible. Keenan slowly sinks into the sofa, his head and hands falling to the cushion.

"Enough, now," Arielle whispers, her lips ghosting along the shell of my ear.

I can feel each of Keenan's heartbeats in my throat, and to be frank, I want to be sure to swallow his very last one. I instinctively push Arielle away from my prey and close my eyes to erase anything but the feel of him dying beneath me. *If only I could taste all of him, then maybe I'd share his special brand of peace and carry it with me forever.*

Two strong arms wrap around my midriff, Arielle's steel grip unwavering as she wrestles me off my mark. "I need more!" I snarl at her, lost in a haze, and her brows pull together. My muscles itch in my arms, more resilient than they used to be, but still no match for her vampire strength.

She drags me to the other end of the room like I'm nothing but a rowdy toddler. "Enough, Leo! He's almost dead."

The distance drills some much-needed awareness back into my foggy brain, and I remember who I am and what I'm doing. My heart swells, a volcano of heat in my chest.

All of a sudden, my shoulder blades itch so painfully that I can't help but scratch at them wildly, digging my nails in my skin, again and again, until it's raw. This new, unexpected torment wrenches out my spine, carving lines deep in my bones, and I cry out in agony.

Arielle tries to stop me from hurting myself, shackling my wrists with her hands.

Tears stream down my face at the pain. "It hurts. I need—Just tear them out of me, please."

Understanding washes over her face. "Turn around."

With both care and decisiveness, my vampire queen peels off the sensitive skin of my back to free my wings. They sprout out of my back and spread out on each side of me, the sharp pain withering down as my body heals itself in one breath, the new appendages now only burning a little.

The feathers are powdery and knitted closely together, and Arielle grazes them with wonder. "By Nyx, you're..."

"He's magnificent," Keenan says from the other side of the room. A lonely tear slides down the angel's cheek, his body stirring weakly on the sofa. "You're...more than I could have hoped for." A sheen of sweat covers his forehead and neck, stressing out exactly how wretched he must be feeling. "Now...I need to rest for a while."

We help him to the bed, the scent of him twisting my insides, and Arielle shakes as she wraps her arms around me. "Thank you for giving me the opportunity to help you through this."

"Thank you for being here."

Shivering in each other's arms, we wonder at each other. I ramble about the shimmering colors in her irises and the freckles on her neck. The impossibly delicate nuances of her skin that I couldn't see with my human eyes... She marvels at the strength of my new body, the birth of my wings, and yet the still familiar scent and warmth she so loves.

For a moment, nothing else exists but us, and while I'm okay with sharing her, I'm glad to have her to myself for a while. And I know, no matter what happens, or the ocean that'll soon separate us, everything will be alright.

# CHAPTER 27
# QUEEN OF KINGS
## ARIELLE

The next morning, I wake up groggy in Leo's arms. The rhythmic loud pounding on the door screams at me that I overslept. "Your Highness, the Prime Minister is heading to your rooms to see you." Bella warns through the closed door, my loyal servant quickly becoming my best confidante.

"How much time do I have?"

"Jude is stalling him as long as he can, but not much."

Damn. It's one thing to be found in bed with both of my lovers, but to be discovered naked in Keenan's bed with both the angels passed out beside me would be harder to explain. I throw on Leo's discarded shirt and scurry down the corridor to Alec's quarters.

I wrench open the door and close it behind me.

"Alec! Are you here?"

I erupt into the nursery, floored to see my deadly bodyguard cradling his nephew to his chest, and the sight warms my body from head to toe. "Good morning," I whisper for the sleeping baby's benefit.

The royal guard hands the baby over to the wet nurse and falls into step with me. "What's going on?"

163

"Get me to my room. The Prime Minister is heading there right now."

Power comes in trenches. The crown. The government. The soldiers. The staff. They all have their own type of power—whether insidious or overstated. The people can only take so much change at a time, and I can't be seen as a hare-brained, ditzy queen that passes out in guest beds without telling anyone about her whereabouts, and the newly appointed Prime Minister is a...compromise. In a show of good faith, I let the government name him to soften the loss of Peter's immense influence on the crown.

Alec and I get into my royal chambers through the back door at the exact same time as the Prime Minister, Axel Brooks, knocks on my door. "My queen, an urgent matter has come to my attention."

"One minute," I answer loudly.

Alec helps me put on my long, velvet queen robe and ties the sash around my waist as Sebastian sits on the bed, a grin landing on his lips.

"Rough night?" my husband asks with a smirk.

He knows I've spent the night with Leo and Keenan, but he's totally getting the wrong idea. "Don't look at me like that. Keenan passed out is all, and I fell asleep in Leo's arms," I say quickly. "That's all."

Both male vampires snort at that, and my mouth opens in outrage. I quickly motion for him to cut it out as I inch the door open.

"The first step toward a new era is to draw a truce with Pereira, so I suggested he should send an emissary, but he decided to come himself—" The interim Prime Minister announces, spooked by Alec's sudden appearance behind me.

My lover raises a brow like he can't quite believe his luck. "Felipe Pereira came himself?"

"Yes."

"To this court?"

"Yes," Axel repeats with a hint of annoyance.

I bite my bottom lip to mask my excitement. "Mr. Beaumont.

Please coordinate security with your brother. Felipe Pereira asked for an audience. We must not disappoint him."

Up until this point, only other species and rebel vampires were held accountable for their mistakes, but that dangerous streak ended with Adele. A wicked gleam dances in Alec's eyes,

"Please arrange for us to meet in an hour. And get the lords and ladies present at court to attend, please," I say quickly.

"An hour, your highness?"

"Yes. I need to change."

He bows at my command.

The audience is quickly arranged, and I have to clench my hands over the armrests of my throne not to pounce at the disgusting king who tried to enslave me forever. His stature is not quite so grand here, his age showing through each and every wrinkle cracking his face, like his black soul is merely contained within his frail body, hollering to get out.

"You... you shouldn't be wearing a crown," Felipe Pereira says to me.

Sebastian leans forward on his throne with a perfectly rehearsed air of boredom. "Look who's talking." His gaze flicks over to Lucas. "Hey, Lulu."

Lucas shudders next to his king, looking absolutely miserable. The gentleman on the king's right must be his Master of War, but I don't remember meeting him before. The bob of Lucas' throat when his gaze spots Leo fills me with warmth.

I offer my guests a genuine smile. "You're here in my home. My kingdom."

*You chose to come, and you must answer to our laws.*

"Your Kingdom owes me reparation for the affront I suffered at your hands, girl."

I bite back the wider grin threatening to surface on my lips, not wanting to give away my current train of thought. "Lucas. Please escort your king to the chapel. I'm sure, given the right incentives, we can all come to an agreement."

How do I know he'll go along with whatever excuse we'll use to explain his king's disappearance? Do I expect him to be on my side because of our history? Our almost life-long friendship?

No.

To my own chagrin, Lucas is a sheep. A sheep I used to think of as my best friend, but a sheep all the same. And I know he'll only back me up on this because I'm the most powerful person in the room.

Maybe in the entire Shadow World.

And in that crypt, I'll make good on my promise to Alec, and make sure that king gets his just deserts.

I have Sebastian and Alec at my side. Leo has promised to return to me after he figures out his place in our world, and Keenan could prove to be a formidable ally. The throne of shadows is mine, and there's a lot to be done.

Vampires all around the world will have to remember why we've been put in charge.

"Long live the Dark Queen," Alec declares to the room, signaling the end of the audience.

A mischievous smile pierces my royal mask as I cross his gaze, the pride he takes in me the most elated emotion I've ever felt.

Sebastian kisses the back of my knuckles, my two angels spread on each side of the staircase, their smooth wings magnificent at their backs, warding off the evil that came knocking at our doors.

"Long live the Dark Queen," the crowd repeats in cheer, my throne as secure as the love I hold for my men. Being their queen is the most sacred destiny of all.

*The End.*

# LOVELY READERS

To support me and the books, please leave a rating or a review on Amazon.

To keep up with my releases and receive exclusive extras, including bonus epilogues and special sneak peeks, join my newsletter.

Click here: http://bit.ly/anyaslair

Xoxo, Anya.

Connect with me on Facebook: https://www.facebook.com/AnyaJCosgrove/

# MAGNETIC: THRONE OF SHADOWS PREQUEL

**Free on KU!**

**Who said life was a fairy tale? Because I'd gladly slice that jerk's head off.**

I'm Vicky, though that's not really my name. Lying becomes second nature when you're on the run.

I never expected to end up half-naked in the woods. I didn't plan to stumble upon the most powerful shifter clan in North America and three of the sexiest men I've ever laid eyes on.

**Dominic, the fun and reckless new wolf.**

**Sam, the hot doctor with glacial-blue eyes.**

**And Gabriel, the intense, secretive alpha who wants nothing to do with me.**

My real name is a one-way ticket back to hell, and my secrets need to stay dead and buried like the girl I used to be.

Sleeping Beauty, Snow White, Red Riding Hood—I can be all three. I can use my powers to earn a place in their werewolf town, away from the bite of my past mistakes. I can use them—and their bodies—to survive.

**The only thing I can't do is fall for them.**

*Magnetic is a stand-alone, steamy reverse harem romance featuring a kick-ass heroine and three swoon-worthy werewolves. Pick up your copy now!*